ABBEVILLE

UNBRIDLED BOOKS

ABBEVILLE

Jack Fuller

Unbridled Books
Denver, Colorado

First paperback edition, 2009
Unbridled Books trade paperback ISBN 978-1-932961-90-4

The Library of Congress has cataloged the hardcover edition as follows:

Fuller, Jack.
Abbeville / by Jack Fuller.
p. cm.
ISBN 978-1-932961-47-8 (hardcover)
ISBN 978-1-932961-90-4 (paperback)
I. Title.
PS3556.U44A63 2008
813'.54dc22

2008000989

1   3   5   7   9   10   8   6   4   2

Book Design by SH • CV

First Printing

This is mortality: to move along a . . . line in a universe where everything, if it moves at all, moves in a cyclical order.

—HANNAH ARENDT

We're a couple of financial wizards.

—GEORGE BAILEY, from *It's a Wonderful Life*

FOR DEBBY
and the memory of Will Tegge

ABBEVILLE

EVEN WHEN I WAS A CHILD, ABBEVILLE seemed too small. It was the kind of place you might have flashed through on a streamliner going somewhere else: a blur of faded paint on plank, a crossing bell rising and falling then gone. Since the last time I'd visited the town, a fire had reduced to rubble the bank my grandfather built, leaving only its walk-in safe standing in the weeds like a crypt. The old grain elevator that had borne Grampa's family name in faded four-foot letters was also gone, replaced by a nameless structure of corrugated steel. No boxcars stood next to it today, but to the north three silver tank cars flashed sun into my eyes. You don't put grain in a tanker. They seemed as out of place in Abbeville as sailing ships.

At least Grampa and Grandma's house had survived, although it had taken on an ugly cladding of vinyl. My mother had sold the place to one of her kin after she'd moved Grandma up to Park Forest to live with us. I'd never thought I would spend another night in it, let alone want to. When I called my second cousin to ask if he had a spare bed, he said I could take my pick because he was going to be away for a month.

"Just go right in," he said. "The door will be open."

"Abbeville is still another world, isn't it," I said.

"Not as much as it used to be," he said.

I didn't stop at the house right away. Instead I took the south crossing over the Chicago and Eastern Illinois tracks. In the local accent, C&EI became See-Nee-Eye. For years I'd thought the name came from an Indian tribe.

Main Street ran parallel to the tracks on the side opposite the house and the unmown prairie along the right-of-way where I used to shoot tin cans off rocks. I drove past the ruins of the bank, then the boarded-up general store. Grampa had owned that at one time, too, along with a number of farms and the implement lot that now held only one rusted old combine, whose delivery assembly poked up out of the weeds like the skull and bony neck of a Brontosaurus.

I rolled on a little way to the north end of Main. The crossing there had a modern set of lights and gates. I wondered why the C&EI had gone to the expense. Everyone in Abbeville knew exactly when each train would pass, as sure as tides.

Crossing the tracks again, I drove back out of town the way I had come. After a couple of miles I turned onto the dirt road that led to the shack Grampa used to own on Otter Creek. Remarkably, it was still standing on the high bank, where you could look out over the lazy current and the marsh beyond. Its plank walls had weathered black, and in a number of places the roof yawned open. The whole structure leaned in the direction of the creek, as if moving water exerted a pull on its timbers the way it always had on Grampa.

He used to love to sit in the beat-up rocker on the porch of the shack, gazing down at the creek. There were no trout in it, and Grampa would not deign to fish with anything but a well-tied fly, so for blood sport he had to settle for smacking pesky sweat bees with a rolled-up section of the *Trib.* He could spend all day like this, contented, insect carcasses piling up, as if bees were money.

When I got out of the car, I half-expected to smell the smoke from his Prince Albert pipe tobacco or to hear him whistling the nine-note, monotone cadence he repeated over and over again like a bird.

Beyond the shack a red-tailed hawk soared over the wide, flat fields. The corn was high. I pulled open an ear to check the quality the way Grampa had taught me. It looked like Abbeville was in store for a pretty fair yield, but any farmer would tell you not to bank on a crop until it was brought in.

I walked the edge of the field, taking in the smell of pollen and leaves and dirt, then returned to the car and drove back to town. On the way I noticed a little trailer sitting on a brick foundation. An American flag flew outside, and next to it somebody had planted a small hand-painted sign that said, "U.S. Post Office." When Grampa delivered the mail, he used the old bank building. He opened it every day but Sunday, as he had when it had served the purpose for which he'd built it. After business hours he would sit in a big old swivel chair with a cracked leather back, tallying the coins he had taken in exchange for postage, accounting sales against revenue again and again down to the last penny.

The garage on Main Street looked to be the only establishment still in business. I pulled in at the ancient pump. The door to the mechanic's bay was open, so I went right in. It had been here that Grampa and the other men had set up a rickety table and played pinochle for matchsticks on Saturday nights. Now the garage smelled only of rubber and oil, but it carried the memory of cigar smoke on Bicycle cards.

"Hello," I called.

A man emerged from the office, drying his hands on a paper towel.

He wasn't as weathered as a farmer, and though he was probably in his thirties, he had the face of a boy.

"I wasn't sure it was self-serve," I said.

A few old tires with new treads lay on the cracked cement floor. When the mechanic finished with the paper towel, he hung it from his hip pocket to dry. In Abbeville using anything only once had always been seen as an extravagance.

"Nice car," said the mechanic.

"It likes the gas a little too much," I said. "But from the look of those tankers on the siding you have plenty."

"You aren't from around here," he said.

"My mother is," I said.

"The tankers don't hold fuel," he said. "They're full of water."

"I was out in one of the fields," I said. "The corn is coming in real sound. It sure didn't seem like a drought."

The mechanic looked at me as if to ask what someone like me would know about judging corn.

"It ain't a matter of weather," he said. "A big corporation bought up pretty much a whole township across the Indiana line, where the soil is real sandy. To make that kind of land produce, they have to run them full-acre sprinkler rigs day and night."

He pointed to a big plastic wastebasket full of water. A ladle hung from its lip.

"By the time the water gets to us," he said, "it stinks of all the chemicals they use."

"I used to love drinking straight from the hand pump," I said. "You had to prime it from a coffee can that sat next to the well. The cement gutter for the runoff was so green with moss it seemed part of the stone."

I followed the young man into the office, fishing in my pocket for cash.

"Should I pay for the gas in advance?" I asked.

He went over and sat down at a desk that looked like it had supported the elbows of a lot of mechanics.

"What did you say your name was?"

"George Bailey," I said.

He smiled.

"My father told me he had a good laugh when your mother gave you that name," he said.

"She had a weakness for *It's a Wonderful Life*," I said.

"Your grandfather's troubles and all," he said.

"And you are?" I said.

"Henry Mueller," said the young man. "My grandfather and yours were good friends. He was Henry, too. Harley Ansel was his nephew, but my grandfather didn't have any use for him after what he done to yours. Go ahead and fill it up."

I pushed open the screen door. They were predicting showers, but there was no sign of them yet. The little vane in the glass bubble on the face of the old pump spun as the gasoline streamed over it, just as it had when my father had filled up his used Ford on Sunday afternoons for the drive back to Park Forest.

"This ought to cover it," I said, coming back through the door and pulling a twenty from my pocket.

"How much was it?" he asked.

"Nineteen seventy-six," I said. "Keep it."

The mechanic pulled open a drawer and rooted around in it for coins.

"There," he said. "We're square."

"I've been thinking about my grandfather a lot lately," I said.

"Some say the bubble busting like it done could bring on another Depression," said the mechanic.

"That's what raised the ghost for me, all right," I said.

"Then you'd better stop trying to pay more than you owe," the mechanic said. "Ask your grandfather's ghost where generosity got him."

I thanked him and took the short drive to the other side of the tracks. As I stepped inside the house the ghost had raised, the air was musty. When Grampa and Grandma lived here, they always had an aromatic fire of corncobs and coal in the cast-iron cookstove. The smell of Grandma's cooking, mixed with Grampa's tobacco, spiced the air.

I have never known anyone who could take such satisfaction in small pleasures as he did: rocking in his chair while cold-smoking a cigar, walking along the edge of a field with me at his side, bellowing out the old German hymns at church in a full basso that knew no sense of pitch whatsoever, or just sitting quietly under a tree at the cemetery. He would sometimes take me there on a clear dawn when the sun was still just below the horizon. He would sit me down, making me move a little this way or a little that until I was just so. "Watch," he would say. "It's Mrs. Hageman's day. The sun's going to rise straight up her cross. Watch." The cemetery was his Stonehenge.

But the rhythms of the world weren't all so benign. Folks who lived close to the land knew full well that they existed at the mercy of these turnings. Nobody understood this better than Grampa. And yet he seemed able to embrace it like providence. I do believe he was the happiest man I have ever known.

My cousin had moved things around and gotten some modern pieces, but many things in the house remained close to the way they had been. Over against one wall stood the huge breakfront that had once held heirloom china that had been brought over from Germany. Now it displayed a careless assortment of dime-store glass. Across the room was the goofy Victorian chair that used to sit just inside the front door. Its high, hard back had coat hooks at the top, which made it look like an instrument of torture.

As I approached the stairs I stopped at the old bookcase with its horizontal glass doors hinged at the top. When I was a boy it had held treasures: Zane Grey's stories for boys, sea tales, a copy of Dale Carnegie and *The Robe,* a number of Bibles, including one inscribed in German in 1851 by one of Grandma's forebears, a leather-bound history of Cobb County, circa 1920, with more than a dozen page numbers listed in the index behind Grampa's name. There was also a secret drawer at the bottom that had held a delegate ribbon from a Republican National Convention long ago, a member's badge from the Chicago Board of Trade, and a silver sheriff's star that at one time in these parts had certified Grampa as the law.

Now the old books were gone, replaced by a collection of *Reader's Digest* condensations. And when I opened the secret compartment, it was empty.

It had never occurred to me that one day I might be wiped out by the market the way Grampa had been. It used to annoy me when my mother would warn me not to get overextended. After all, I was an accomplished man. Trained in the best schools. And by the time the technology boom came along, I had already been in business long enough to have seen my share of ups and downs. In fact, I used to argue from good, University of Chicago financial theory that we needed more diversity in our firm's portfolio. But at some point money becomes a tsunami sweeping away everything, starting with theory. And the dot-com wave was bigger than anyone had ever seen.

A computer terminal on the credenza in my office kept me plugged directly into the swells. They called it a Bloomberg after the man who had started the company. Thanks to his machine, I had instantaneous access to every significant market on the planet. I'd programmed my Bloomberg to display the stocks our venture capital firm had seen through their initial public offering, plus the securities I owned outside the partnership.

I loved my Bloomberg. Sure, there were days when the screen shone a little too red, its way of denoting a falling price. But the technology boom was creating wealth at such an astonishing rate that most days the screen glowed as blue as a harvest sky.

One of the reasons I did not take my mother's financial admonitions seriously was that I never felt I was living anywhere close to the way I could have. We had a lovely house near the lake, but in Wilmette, not Winnetka or Lake Forest. I drove a nice car, a Lexus, and Julie had an Audi. But there were no Ferraris or Lotuses in our garage. Not even a BMW Z3 to tool around in on the weekends. Yes, we did have our son in North Shore Country Day School, which was pricey. But it was a better fit for him than the public schools. And we did extend ourselves philanthropically, which led to invitations to join several cultural and educational boards. Certainly we enjoyed some benefit, though happily none that the IRS would say required us to reduce the amount of our gift we could deduct. I'm talking about dinner parties with interesting or well-connected people and black-tie social events that, frankly, Julie got much more out of than I did.

The day everything changed followed one such benefit. I forget what kind of human suffering it was for. Julie and I had set the alarm a little later than usual and over breakfast enjoyed a little conversation about whatever the *Trib* had on its front page. Then Julie motivated Rob out of bed as I suited up. We all left at the same time, Julie to drive Rob to school (he was a year shy of getting his driver's license) and I to head down Sheridan Road to Lake Shore Drive, then eventually turn inland to the office building where I worked.

When I got to my desk, I did my e-mail, made a few calls, and worked on my in-box. At 10 a group of young men fresh from the best business schools pitched several of my partners and me on backing their startup company. They dressed in chinos and Façonnable shirts with the top two buttons open to show tanned, hairless chests.

By the time I arrived, the delegation had already been served four-dollar water, and its members had arrayed themselves at the big table so that the people from my firm would have to sit interspersed among them. In the trade this was known as boy-girl-boy-girl.

"Great to see you," said the apparent leader. "John Durkin."

"Hi, John. Bill Brewer."

"Hi, Bill."

"Thad Reiner."

"Thad. Bill Brewer."

"Bill."

The purpose of the ritual was to imprint each new name in the cranial Contacts file.

"Sid Benz."

"Sid. Bill Brewer."

"Bill."

Their proposition had some appeal, and after a short conference with my partners in the hall, we invited them to come back later in the week to give us more financial detail. We did not say it that way, of course, because dwelling on financials was passé. Instead, Brewer explained to them that we wanted "a little more granularity." To which the leader of the fledgling company said, "Got it," as if he had just solved a problem in linear programming.

Next I was off to lunch with an old friend who had made a bundle in computer consulting. According to the argot of the day, he "sold shovels," which alluded to the strategy a risk-averse businessman might adopt during a gold rush. Caution notwithstanding, my friend had a catholic curiosity and a penetrating mind, which always led to interesting conversation. This day he reported that he had been reading about the Cambrian Explosion, a period in the evolution of life on Earth when suddenly an enormous profusion of new species emerged in the sea. His interest was not random, since the Cambrian Explosion had come to be a metaphor for the extraordinary multiplicity of new products and services offered up by Internet entrepreneurs.

"If we had been there," he said, "I imagine we would have bet on the most complex, bright, and beautiful creatures. But do you know which had the greatest odds of survival? Slugs and worms. They did not fight the current. They let themselves be carried along."

I told him he was just trying to justify sticking to the shovels.

"You do what you can," he said, smiling as he picked up the check.

The moment I returned to the office, I realized something was happening. All the secretaries were away from their desks. The place was so silent it reminded me of the way the air in Abbeville felt just before a tornado. I went to my desk. The Bloomberg was drenched in blood.

Down. Down. Everything was down. Dot-com stocks and other tech-sector securities were taking the worst beating, but even the index funds and the blue chips were bleeding. It was a rout.

Late in the day Jim Bishop, the firm's founding partner, called an all-hands meeting.

"Corrections get corrected," he said, full of patrician confidence. "This, too, shall pass."

Unfortunately, it did not. The market kept falling. Young entrepreneurs who had been worth hundreds of millions of dollars on paper were suddenly worth no more than the recycle value of the paper. Companies that had been the market's darlings sent out broadcast e-mails to their employees, informing them that their jobs no longer existed.

Partners' draws at Bishop & Dodge went to zero as the firm attempted to preserve its capital. I was able to turn a few of the securities in my private account into cash so I could continue to pay the bills. Nothing else was liquid unless I was willing to lose a hundred dollars to get one. At some point my equity in the firm sank below the equity we had in our home.

Even though I would ordinarily have preferred to spare Julie, the situation was so grave that I had to talk to her. As I explained our circumstances, she looked at me with such trusting eyes that I thought the full import of the news was not penetrating.

Then she said, "Are we in trouble?"

"Everybody we know is," I said.

In the weeks that followed, a feeling of utter helplessness came over me. I tried to take measures to economize, such as shopping for groceries armed with coupons from the Sunday paper. I cut them out in my office; there was not much else to do there. Meantime, I put feelers out to a number of commercial banks, hungering for a proper salary again, no matter how modest. I never received so much as an e-mail in reply.

All the while the memory of Grampa kept coming back to me, and eventually I decided I had to return to Abbeville.

I climbed the stairs to the second floor of the big old house where he had spent most of his life. The steps still creaked in the same places they had when I was a boy. The hall at the top was still a gallery of portraits. Large, ceremonial photographs looked down, the ones that had seemed to sit in judgment of me during my adolescent years. Over there were Grandma's parents, looking fresh off the boat. Next to them Grampa and Grandma themselves, probably barely into their twenties, as relaxed as a neck brace. I went to the bedroom where I had always slept, hung my garment bag in the armoire, slipped off my shoes, and lay down on the big, white-painted iron bed. The feather mattress enveloped me. At some point I heard ticking from downstairs. My cousin must have thought to have someone come in and wind the heavy ceramic clock that had chimed every hour I had spent in Abbeville.

I quickly drifted off to sleep and dreamt of fleeing something I could not name. When I awakened, the crossing bells were calling the approach of a train. My legs slid off the bed. The whole house began to rumble, a tremor of the earth.

Tiny raindrops were gathering on the rattling window. I slipped my shoes back on, got my Gore-Tex jacket and a pair of rubber over-shoes from my bag, and went downstairs. When I pulled the car up to the crossing, I looked down the tracks at the retreating lights of the caboose, port and starboard. The whistle fell as if being borne into the past.

As I drove by the church, I felt a little pang as I recalled the time I had broken a stained-glass window. Then the town fell away, and the flat, endless fields spread out on either side of me. At the rutted road to the cemetery I turned and bounced up a slight incline to what Grampa used to say was the highest point in Cobb County. He should have known, since he had been the one to fence it in when his father had donated the land.

It wasn't hard to locate my father's grave, even though I had not visited it often during the twenty years since we had buried him. He lay near the back fence with the extended family: the Schumpeters, the Vogels, and assorted others. This was my mother's choice. She wanted us all to be together in the end. When she talked about this to my father, his Irish came out. He said that being planted in Abbeville was fine with him; he was pretty sure he'd have nowhere better to go.

I had always changed the subject when my mother started going into her ultimate plans for Julie and me. But now I found it reassuring that our plots were in a trust my mother had established, so there would always be at least one asset left.

My father's gravestone was flat to the ground. In fact, it seemed a little sunken, perhaps the effect of the disturbed water table. Behind it stood a small plastic American flag in a VFW holder with his World War II rank (sergeant) and dates of service (1940–1945). I got down on one knee and soon found myself speaking aloud.

"I tried my best," I told him. "But everything is falling apart."

Then a memory rose from the dead. From kindergarten we had drilled for nuclear war so much that it had become a wolf cried too often. But then came the Cuban Missile Crisis, and suddenly the beast was at the door. I was sure that soon I would hear the sirens pierce the air, and all I would be able to do would be to count down the seconds until all life expired.

In the midst of it my father came into my bedroom one night as I tried to go to sleep.

"It is probably hard for you to believe," he said, "but I have known some of what you are feeling. A lot of things happen in this life of ours. Some are very personal. Some are so big it's no wonder folks attribute them to the devil or the wrath of God. This country has been through hell. Most of it probably seems long ago to you, but some of the worst happened not much before you were born. The Depression. Pearl Harbor. There were times that made me wonder how we'd ever get through. But we did. Or at least most of us did. Life does go on, George. It always does."

With the Cold War over now, at least my son didn't have to live with the nightmare of death hurtling out of the sky. For my father, of course, it hadn't been a dream. When the kamikazes aimed their Zeros at his troop ship, he was as awake as a man can be.

I stood up at his grave. The drizzle had stopped, and the sun came heavily lidded beneath the far edge of the clouds near the horizon. Off to the right rose the monument with Grampa and Grandma's names on it, along with their dead infant son. It was imposing in such a small place; Grampa must have bought it when he was still flush. It had ample room for his father's and mother's names, his brother's as well, Grampa's act of unconditional, unaccountable love for a man who had led him into disaster.

I stood before the monument for a time. The limestone angels had lost their faces to the wind and rain, the point of the obelisk gone as dull as a worn pencil. I tried getting down on my knees again, but this time no words came. I did not know where to begin.

2

THE DRY, GRAY EARTH CRACKED UNDER THE blade. Every inch came hard. It would have been much easier to put in these fence posts in April, when the rain-dampened soil had been as black as night and the weeds had not yet woven their roots into a shield. But nobody had needed burying in the spring.

The young man looked over the patch of ground he was supposed to enclose. A generous amount, more than three acres, it seemed absurdly large for the purpose, especially since his father had given him posts—which seemed as big around as tree trunks—on which to string wire delineating exactly what he had donated and what he had not.

Old Rolf Schlagel was going to be mighty lonely up here. Eventually, of course, he'd have company. But the young man, in a collarless, hand-me-down Sunday shirt that had been worn to patches under his father's only suit, could not imagine it ever filling up.

When his father had given the land, memorializing it in several stiffly worded documents in his perfect Germanic hand, he had held back twenty plots for his immediate family. Twenty! There were only four of them in Abbeville: Mother and Father, himself, and his brother, Friedrich. Twenty plots would take the Schumpeters into the next millennium, which seemed to a young man as distant as the last.

Karl took out his blue bandanna and wiped his face, then the band of his straw hat. A little breeze would be all right about now. Or somebody stopping by to lend a hand. But he supposed that everybody was at the crick, swimming or fishing for the big cats that lived on the mud. Probably getting a laugh at his expense, too: fencing in ghosts, eh? That barbed wire better be mighty sharp.

His father's plan was to have the job done before they planted old Rolf on Saturday. That meant putting in every post today, then wrestling with the wire tomorrow, giving himself a day to spare in case of weather. As his father always reminded him, "I've never once known anyone to win an argument against the rain." Nor against Karl's father either. Stubborn as this fence pole, and sometimes twice as thick.

Karl dug deep to anchor the fence against the upthrust of the winter freeze. When he got a post situated, he filled in around it and stomped on the soil until the ground was tight.

Sometimes after a day's labor was done, he rode off on a horse and did not return until past the hour when everyone in Abbeville was in bed. Folks said it must be rutting season. But if that were it, he would simply have found a gypsy woman, who the boys said would touch you anywhere you wanted for a price. And anyway, he saved his fancy for a respectable girl, Cristina Vogel, whose father farmed a spread a mile west of the Schumpeters'. Karl was not alone in his interest. Harley Ansel, who was a year younger than Karl and a year older than Cristina, clearly had hopes for her as well. Karl did not have much experience with the way the opposite sex saw things, but he felt sure Cristina would not reciprocate Ansel's attentions. The boy had a jagged edge that did not come from breaking earth.

A fence does not get built this way, Karl thought. It was foolish to drive oneself idle with ideas. But whenever he saw the gypsies crossing the prairie in their strange caravans—not living by the rhythm of the seasons but cutting straight through them toward something beyond—he could not help wondering what they aimed to find.

He increased the vigor of his digging until the hole reached the proper depth, then slid a post from the back of the horse cart. His father had felled it and stripped it of its bark, but he had left the bulbous knots where the limbs had been, which gave the post the look of a prehistoric bone. Karl thought of trying to hoist it to his shoulder, but the distance to the hole was short, so it was easier just to drag it.

The bottom end scraped along, seeming to get hung up on every stone, but eventually he got it to the lip of the hole and heaved it vertical so that he could get around it with both arms. It slid down his front haltingly. Knots tugged at his belt. Finally it hit bottom, sending a shudder up through him. He had to look around to make sure no one coming up from town had seen him dancing and thrusting as if he were a dog on somebody's leg.

Karl scraped the piles of fertile earth back into the hole with his boot, then began to stomp it down. There were girls at the barn dances in the Coliseum who would let you brush up against them ever so briefly as you wheeled by in the square. You could feel the softness of them, but even the most wanton permitted no more than this. And if a boy ever did manage to lure one of them outside, he found the farmers out there waiting for them, smoking their pipes in the dark like sentries.

Cristina was not such a girl. She had a dignity and seriousness of purpose far beyond her years. He was sure she was the kind who would let only one man touch her, the one she decided to wed.

Work, Karl. Work. The wind had picked up enough that when he lifted the next post, he had to take it into account. More shoulder and less embrace made this encounter a mite less incriminating. The post slid down the shallow trough he had cut to make the process easier. When he had one whole side completed, he checked the alignment: as straight as the numbers in one of his father's ledgers.

The wind blew his sweat cold as he admired his work with the devil's pride. The proper antidote, of course, was the same as for desire: redoubled labor. He worked steadily through the afternoon until, with three sides of the rectangle complete and the fourth started, Friedrich showed up, collar and hair still wet from the crick.

"Do any good today?" Karl asked.

"Robert got him a few," said Fritz. "Fat ones, too."

"See any water moccasins?" Karl asked.

"Naw," said Fritz, as if it wouldn't have scared the bejabbers out of him if he had.

"Were you the only two there?" Karl asked.

"Andrew Schwarz and Harley Ansel came later," Fritz said.

"Harley give you any trouble?" Karl asked.

"Naw," said Fritz. "When I told him what you was doing, it gave him a good enough laugh that I guess it satisfied him."

"Don't ever let him bully you," Karl said. "I'll have a talk with him if you need me to."

"Aw, Harley ain't so bad," Fritz said, and Karl could not help thinking that Fritz had probably laughed right along with him.

He went to the horse cart to pull down another post from the dwindling pile.

"I'll help," said Fritz.

Karl could have asked his father to assign Fritz to assist him, but it was the elder's lot to shoulder the burden.

"Dad sure did give them enough land," said Fritz, gazing down the long-side fencerow.

"Got to last till Judgment Day, I guess," said Karl.

The younger boy walked over to the empty hole and looked down. The wind had abated, and bees flitted at the dandelions.

"You suppose he's fixing to bury himself here?" said Fritz.

"He'll probably be looking for a little help from the two of us," said Karl.

"I mean him and Ma, they'll both be here?"

"Don't get too far ahead of yourself, Fritz," said Karl.

As he began to lift the next post from the pile, Fritz leaped to help.

"It's all right," said Karl. "I got it."

Fritz disregarded Karl and managed to get the butt end off the ground. The quiver of his exertion expressed itself down the whole length of the log.

"Steady, boy," Karl said.

That only made the log wobble so much that Karl could feel it working out of his own grasp.

"Just let me know if you're going to have to drop it, Fritz," he said, using all his will to keep up his end for fear that if he lost it, the weight would crush his brother's hands.

Without warning Fritz simply let go. This broke Karl's grip, and the heavy log crashed against his shin.

"Almighty!" he cried as he went down.

The pain did not come immediately, but when it did, it radiated from the spot of the blow upward and downward until it hurt as much as a part of him could.

As he held his shin between his hands, the feeling began to center itself where he could test it. When he realized that the wound was more likely a bruise than a break, the question of Fritz began to intrude into his selfish pain.

He was nowhere to be seen from the ground where Karl lay curled.

Karl straightened his leg against the hurt, rolled off his hip, and pushed himself upward to a sitting position. It was only then that he saw the retreating form. Fritz's impulse to flee was as much a part of his nature as a rabbit's.

Karl leaned on an arm opposite the injury and pushed up against the burden of the earth. When he got upright he listed, but he was able to stand.

"Fritz!" he called out, waving his arms. "It's all right."

Fritz turned, but trouble was trouble, and it never went away. So you had to. Just that simple, said the rabbit.

Karl's leg ached something fierce. It gave him sharp notice whenever he put too much weight on it. But still he found that if he stood correctly, canted away from the weak side so he could take the burden on his good leg, he could still lift. It did test his back, but no more than hay bales in tight quarters in the loft. He used the tool to brace himself as he leaned over, then used the pole itself for balance as he slid it.

Getting the fence post upright proved to be another matter. He pushed his bad leg as far as he could, but still the angle was wrong. The log would not slide into place. It began to wobble, and he had to throw it from him. At this point he really could have used his brother's help. But that was an idle thought. He tried again and again until he succeeded. Eventually he was able to master how to work hurt so he could keep going until the posts turned the empty land sacred.

There had been jeopardy, but he had gotten through it. Danger was always present, whether in building a fence or running the sharp-bladed implements in the fields. It was there even in pleasure, climbing a tall lookout tree near the crick or touching a girl at the dance who you could tell wanted to come back around to be touched again.

It was the way of the world to put obstacles in the path between a man and the things he wanted or was obliged to do. Otherwise, Karl supposed, a soul would never be measured. Maybe this then was the reason God made moccasin snakes and swimming holes and gypsy women and little brothers.

3

WHEN KARL LIMPED INTO THE HOUSE, he did not mention Fritz's role in his injury. He had just lost his balance, he said.

"That is the cause of all human misery," Karl's father observed.

Karl could think of quite a few other causes—starting with severe fathers—but he stood silently, wondering what punishment his father would mete out to him for a job well done.

His father began to pace.

"Success in agriculture today takes more than a knee for the weather," he said.

Was this a test? It was not his knee that he had hurt.

"Your mother and I have decided." His father stopped and straightened himself at every joint, as if he were lifting whatever it was he was trying to say. Then he finally spoke again. "It is time you were exposed to the world."

Karl's mind leaped up. Chicago. Grain and livestock pouring in from all over the plains. He could hear the animals' frightened cries, see throngs of people as numberless as the Bible's multitudes.

"You will be going to the North Woods to work with your uncle," his father said.

It was as if Karl had been tackled and brought to earth.

"Why send me so far?" he complained. "What do I need to know of the forest?"

"He is my brother," his father said.

KARL WENT BY TRAIN, switching lines he forgot how many times, until he found himself in a freezing boxcar with a dozen ruffians who, to his dismay, all got out at the same bleak rail crossing he did. From there they were taken by open oxcart mile upon bumpy mile until they reached a scar in the forest that turned out to be the camp of Schumpeter Logging Co.

"Looking for something?" said the enormous oxcart driver, his words clotted by an accent that was not German but more German than French.

"I'm to meet Mr. John Schumpeter," Karl said. "I'm to be working for him."

"Everybody does that," said the ox man.

"I'm to be his clerk," Karl said.

"Be you a saw clerk or a wagon clerk?" said the ox man.

"Ledger clerk," said Karl, who could only guess at the penalty for a smart mouth. "I'm to learn the business from him."

"You'll learn a lot more than that here," said the ox man. Then his thick finger pointed toward the other side of the camp. "A person can usually find Mr. Schumpeter over to that big old pile of logs they call the office. But usually you don't go there unless he asks you to, and then you'd usually just as rather not. By the way, Mr. Ledger Clerk, be sure to wipe those boots off afore you enter. Mr. Schumpeter lives in that office of his, and he likes to keep it as neat as Astor Street. You know where that is, don't you?"

"No," said Karl.

"And you never will neither."

With that the ox man turned away, and Karl struck out across the muddy yard. The first log structure he reached smelled like a kitchen. He poked his head inside, barely able to make out anything except for the glow of coals in a fireplace under a hanging cauldron straight out of the Brothers Grimm.

"I'm looking for Mr. Schumpeter," said Karl.

"I look like him to you?"

"I've never laid eyes on him," said Karl.

He put the wind in his face again and slogged toward a cabin that looked a cut or two nicer than the rest. He knocked tentatively on the jamb of the open door.

"Hello?" he said.

From inside came the scrape of a chair, then heavy footsteps on wooden planking. When the figure appeared in the rectangle of light from the doorway, it was . . . his father!

The shock lasted only an instant. Then he noticed the age lines, the rounder jaw.

"I'm Emil's son," Karl said.

"I was worried that he had decided not to let you come after all," said Uncle John, reaching out his hand. "He went this way and that way for months after I suggested it."

Uncle John wore heavy work clothes. But you could tell he was not a man of common labor. His grip would not have held a bucking horse, perhaps the effect of having so many saw clerks and ox clerks.

Karl's first lesson in business came the very next day, the basics of double-entry bookkeeping. He was not so sure at first about doing everything twice, but his uncle did not seem to be one to waste motion. For one thing, he did not repeat himself, unlike Karl's father, who assumed his sons could never harvest anything clean on a single pass.

Soon Karl began to appreciate the ways of the account books. He learned to make the figures tell the future, not like a gypsy lady, but scientifically: Let this number drift upward—by paying the men too generously or buying too many provisions—and that number (net profits) began to drop. Your fortune, or the loss of it, was not in the Tarot cards or crystal ball; it was right there on the ledger paper.

He lived with Uncle John in the back of the main cabin. At night Karl would watch his uncle poring over the dense market tables in the *Chicago Tribune*, a packet of which was delivered once a week. He did not know what his uncle was looking for, but somebody could have detonated a stick of dynamite outside and Uncle John would not have lost his place.

Meantime, Karl began to admire the men he at first had feared. He came to love the forests and streams in which they worked, learned to find his way by moss and the lay of shadows. He developed a genuine feel for the contours of sand hill and swamp. He soon knew the names of birds and the melodies of their songs. He could track deer and turkey. More than once, during slack times in the office, Uncle John let him go off with scouts to investigate virgin lands they intended to work during the winter.

It was on one of these journeys that he came across the river that drew him for the rest of his days. Ahead of them a big buck turned and stared at them for a moment before cracking off into the deep brush. As they reached the lowlands, their boots began to sink into the wet loam, the suck of their footsteps punctuating the hush of invisible waters and the rustle of the wind.

Suddenly off to Karl's right something reared up. He turned. It was a bear, and it had a cub.

Karl froze. The others, who had not seen it, continued to move up behind him.

He had never known such an animal. On the farm there were weasels and coyotes, but they wanted to stay away from you. The bear stood its ground.

The cub kept rooting around, curious about everything. At some point it began to edge in Karl's direction and would not retreat. Karl did not dare move because mama had one clear purpose, and it was as old as life. When her child came closer to Karl and mama showed her fangs, Karl's foot found a stiff twig and snapped it to back off the cub. We're in this together, little cub, Karl thought. A tremor went through the mother.

Then from behind him came a shot. The shot was clean. The mama bear's legs buckled and she fell.

Her cub went to her and began poking her with its snout. The next bullet came so close that Karl could hear it ticking through the branches near his ear. The cub collapsed.

A sharp cry pierced the forest. It did not come from the animal.

The ox man and the Norwegian with the rifle ran to him.

"You hurt?" shouted the ox man, who went by the name of Peter Hoekstra.

"Big one," said the Norwegian, grinning. He moved up to the carcasses and touched the mama's nose with his toe to make sure she was gone.

Karl had been around butchering all his life, so he knew what to do. When he finished flaying the beasts for their skins, he waded into the river to consecrate it with the blood from his hands and to cool in himself the heat that blood had raised.

Though the mortal teachings of the forest were not over for the day, at least the next lesson brought with it a measure of grace: Hoekstra had decided the time had come to show Karl how to cast a fly.

The Dutchman began the process by opening a case and drawing from it the thin reed of a long, delicate rod. He assembled it and attached a small reel. With big, blunt fingers he tied together some lengths of light gut until it tapered down so fine that Karl could not imagine it being able to hold anything wild. Then suddenly Hoekstra reached up and snatched something from the air. As he slowly opened his hand, Karl saw a grasshopper, disoriented, taking a few tentative steps.

Carefully, Hoekstra stuck the body though with a needle-sharp hook that he had clenched to the end of his line with a series of brisk, perfect movements. The hopper was still alive, beating madly against the awful weight it suddenly bore. The Dutchman stood, released it from his hand, and in one smooth motion snapped the line back behind him. The moment it had completely unfurled, he shot it forward again, laying it out across the water as straight as a saw blade.

This first cast went about halfway across the river so that the fly landed at the upstream edge of a piece of flat water. The Dutchman stepped farther out into the current until he was up to his knees. Karl followed, and cold water filled his boots as the hopper drifted downstream, twitching.

The Dutchman lifted the line off the water in one sweeping pull. Karl followed the fly backward through its long, beautiful loop, then forward again until it fell just an inch short of a half-submerged log along the opposite bank.

"Ah," said Hoekstra.

Karl thought it was because he had almost hooked the log, but then a large silver shape darted from beneath it. The water swirled and the hopper was gone.

The Dutchman lifted the rod tip. There was an instant of pure suspended time before the fish came alive to its peril. It knew how to protect itself from blue heron and eagle. It knew to stay clear of otters. It only came out in the open to feed when it felt secure. But it had surely never felt the sting of sharpened iron.

Hoekstra held the tip of the rod high and let the line hiss out through the guides. At some point, as the fish raced toward a tangle of fallen limbs downstream, he put his palm to the reel and slowed it down. The rod bent under the force of the fish in the current, which grew stronger against Karl's legs as he followed the Dutchman down-river.

"Here," said Hoekstra, handing him the rod. "Now you kill something."

Pure wildness pulled at Karl as he felt the fish's desperate struggle against what was written for it on the waters.

"What do I do now?" he said.

The Dutchman signaled Karl with a circular motion as the line grew slack. Karl understood that he should begin to reel in.

The fish had turned under the pressure and now was moving by fits and starts back upstream toward them. Karl reeled in as fast as he could to keep the line taut so the hook stayed deep in the fish's jaw. Finally the rod tip bent again and shook. For a moment the fish appeared on the water's surface.

"Lordy," Karl said.

"Good fish," said the Dutchman.

It had to be more than two feet long, as big as a catfish on Otter Creek but ten times as strong.

A smile came to Karl's lips, then vanished.

It was as if a gale had suddenly gone dead or every bird in the woods had hushed at once. All the tension had gone out of the line.

"You tried to use your strength," said Hoekstra. "The fish used it against you."

"I'm sorry," said Karl.

"You will learn," said the Dutchman. "That is the difference between you and the fish. For you and me, most mistakes don't kill us."

The Dutchman rerigged the line, using an artificial fly this time, tied with what looked like deer hair and feathers. He showed Karl how to use the weight of the line and the spring of the bamboo to throw this tiny, weightless thing. Soon Karl was getting it out far enough that the fly drifted naturally in the current. Then, bang, another fish took. This time Karl was more patient and landed it. It was not such a fine fish as the first, but this one was all his. He struck its head on a rock, then laid it out on the grass of the bank.

"We'll fill our bellies with grayling tonight," Hoekstra said.

Karl nodded, but his stomach was the least of it. He felt as though he had touched something fundamental, something that could be found only in cold, moving waters and the other wild things of the world.

4

WHEN THE FIRST FROST CAME, THE CAMP
began to fill up with men. By then the
scouting parties had investigated tens of thousands of acres along either
bank of the river, reaching the end of the Indian claim in all directions.
A master map in Uncle John's cabin marked all the best stands of forest, but the locations of the prime fishing holes were marked only in
the hidden memories of the men who had found them.

Once the ground stiffened, the lumberjacks began bringing down
the tall trees with two-man crosscut saws, then stripping their branches
with axes. It was incredible how quickly they could harvest what had
taken centuries to produce.

Ordinarily, Uncle John had said, they would pile the logs on top of
a frozen river, ready to float down to the sawmills along the lake when
spring came. But here the river never completely froze, so the logs had
to be arranged along the water's edge waiting to be rolled in when the
season changed and the snow melt-off swelled the current. The river
did not freeze because underground springs warmed it. If you stood

on a high bank in certain places and looked straight down into the clear water, you could see the sand billowing upward, like smoke from a fire at the center of the earth.

Uncle John had been absent most of the fall. For him logging was a sideline; his real business was in Chicago. Karl kept in touch with him by packet, which went out by rail or across the lake by boat. Then one frigid day in December Uncle John reappeared. The first thing he did was look at Karl's books.

"Don't you want to go to the river and see what we've produced?" Karl asked.

"Right now the actual logs are deadweight," said his uncle. "They only become important when they have been reduced thus." He tapped the columns with his forefinger.

"Reduced to money," said Karl.

"Or any other counter that seems appropriate: tons, board feet, shiploads," said Uncle John. "I do this work out of affection now. Or better, perhaps, out of habit, which is what becomes of affection over time. You are young, so you do not yet see how one thing so easily transforms into another."

"Cone to tree," said Karl. "Tree to house."

They were seated next to one another at the desk, the ledger between them. As his uncle spoke, he looked out the door, where water dripped from the roof and the sun was cold on the gray mixture of snow and sand that covered the ground.

"Most of my business is even purer of the physical," he said. "I suppose I do come to the woods to renew my connection with what you can touch. Maybe we should go down to the river now, the two of us, and distract ourselves with reality for a bit."

The Indian claim stretched twenty miles east to west and ten north to south, a perfectly drawn bureaucratic rectangle laid upon the vast sand hills covered with white pine and lowland marshes rich with game. From the crest of a hill you could sometimes discern the curve of the land, but most of the time the sheer profusion of trees obscured it. Uncle John said it was one of the few such parcels of timberland still left that was located on a river good enough to carry the harvest to market.

"There's one of the braves," said Karl.

Across the river, in a thick stand of trees, he could just make out the form of a young man. Often one or two of them would appear out of the forests, look on from the shadows for a time, then disappear.

Karl and his uncle walked along a path that took them past stacks of logs secured with great stakes driven through the frost. In the spring when the ground softened, the logs would be loosed with a few decisive strokes of the sledgehammer.

"We have done a lot in your absence," said Karl.

"This is only the beginning," said Uncle John. "We will have to fell a hundred times this just to cover the costs."

"The river will choke," said Karl.

"Yes," Uncle John said.

He stayed less than a week. Under Hoekstra's tutelage Karl had become good enough with the oxcart to be trusted to drive his uncle back to the train crossing. A fog was coming up from the ground. The snow weighed upon the boughs, and occasionally one shuddered and dropped a pillow to the ground.

The train had only one car and no other passengers. Uncle John mounted the steps, and Karl handed up his canvas bag and leather briefcase.

"Will you be back?" Karl asked.

"When we are ready to commit our fortunes to the river," Uncle John said. "Then you shall really see something."

. . .

WINTER DEEPENED, AND THOUSANDS upon thousands of acres of pine came down as the crews relentlessly pushed from the river outward. Log piles grew into great pyramids along the water's edge. Hoekstra's beard of ice made him look like the Sphinx.

Even though Karl did his bookwork at a desk warm inside the cabin, he gathered his data outside. He became used to the bitter chill but often wished his duties required more exertion.

Logging was much more dangerous than farming. Trees fell erratically and broke bones. One tall pine took an eccentric bounce off the branches of another on the way down and crushed a man's skull. Still, the perils of winter—with its frostbite, icy footing, falling oxen, brittle skin, and thunderous collapse of trees—turned out to be nothing compared with what happened when the snow began to melt and the river rose.

It was uncanny that Uncle John managed to reappear just before the thaw. Karl had known farmers who could feel the weather coming, but not from a distance of hundreds of miles. Two days after Uncle John arrived, the temperature rose to almost 50 and the icicles began to fall from cabin eaves like spears.

For as far as the eye could see they had taken the forest down to stumps and underbrush. You did not find many animals except the occasional rodent or milk snake. The river seemed to have become nothing more than a machine for transport. Karl wondered how any fish could possibly have survived.

In his cabin Uncle John put down the ledger and stretched out his hands on either side of it.

"If you would like," he said, "I will try to persuade your father that a business education should not end in the North Woods."

"He won't want to hear that," Karl said.

"Shall we have a look at the preparations?" Uncle John said.

The land seemed more barren than a cornfield after harvest. The only places that remained untouched were the bottomland swamps, which were nothing but rot.

"Will we replant?" Karl asked.

"A good farmer's question," said his uncle. "But there is no reason to cultivate trees here. Since the coming of the railroads, the rivers are now made of steel; any kind of tree floats on them. This means the price of white pine is dropping, and it will never rise again."

"What will happen?"

"The forest will regenerate," said his uncle. He pointed to a chipmunk rooting around in a pile of brush. "In the meantime, if there is food for him here, he will stay and prosper. If not, he will either move on or die. It is the same for us."

As they approached the water, the noise increased. Men barked orders. Chains clanked. Wood rasped against wood. Out of the reeds stepped a dark figure soaked to the skin. In the still air his clothing actually steamed.

"Goddamn greenhorn!" he said. "Ran a goddamn log right over mine."

The river was engorged with melted snow. Two lumberjacks knocked away the stays at a rollway, and the logs thundered down the bank and hit the water like an explosion. The men stood and watched silently, as if it were a natural disaster.

When the logs in the river stopped moving forward, the lumberjacks stripped down to their undershirts and walked out onto the treacherous jams, their only protection an uncanny sense of balance and a safety rope, which seemed just as likely to get snagged and pull them under as to provide for their rescue. Armed with long, pike-like peavies, they attempted by applying leverage to unlock the front logs and set them parallel with the current, which rushed under them in a torrent.

Hoekstra picked his way surely from log to angled log. He was an enormous man, and his very bulk caused movement in the jam. Fortunately for the Dutchman, it was not enough to break the mess apart because if that happened without his being ready, he would be crushed to death.

He moved quickly toward the center until he found the keystone logs. They were fast against a half-sunken stump that backed up against a boulder that held it firm. After surveying the situation, he slipped back to the rear end of one of the leading logs and jumped. The height of his leap took Karl's breath. The Dutchman landed on both feet, his outstretched arms angling to hold his balance. The shuddering log bucked but did not break free.

Dozens of other lumberjacks watched from the banks. Hoekstra walked forward again and surveyed the geometry. Then suddenly he undid the safety rope from his waist and plunged into the icy water. In unison the crowd drew a breath. For a moment Karl could see his head just above the water. Then it disappeared. Seconds passed. A minute. Two lumberjacks took a step out onto the jam, then backed off. Something was happening. At first it was just a nervousness among the logs. Then came an awful groan that could have been a man's death agony amplified a thousand times. Hoekstra's head popped out the water. Foam flew from his hair, and with both arms he hugged the lead log as it slowly gave way.

The safety rope lay useless across the top of the jam, which was all in motion now. Someone retrieved the rope and tried to throw a loop to him. But it was too late. The log he was holding careered downstream a few feet ahead of the others. He struggled with it like a man wrestling a beast.

At the next bend the river narrowed, deepened, and went flat. Karl knew the spot well because several times while fishing he had been sucked down into the cavernous hole. It was a place a man could die.

But the deeper, slacker water was just what the Dutchman wanted because in it the log slowed down enough that he was able to guide it shoreward. Then in one terrible moment he made a leap to a spot just behind a fallen tree, which held off the tumbling logs for a couple of seconds before snapping like a twig. By then Hoekstra had clambered up the bank and was looking back at the crushing weight of the harvest as it swept past him.

That night Karl and his uncle sat across from one another eating dinner.

"Dangerous business out there today," said Karl.

"Without risk, there is no business," said Uncle John, wiping his lips on a handkerchief. "You borrow money to buy rights to a territory, hire a skeleton crew in the summer to scout it. Then you wait for the freeze. If it comes late, you lose precious days. If the snow doesn't fall, the rivers don't rise in the spring to float the logs. These things are variable, but the interest on that borrowed money is as relentless as the current. Many have drowned."

"It seems a shame to have to borrow," said Karl, his father's son.

"The need for capital is what has kept every lumberjack out here from going into business against me," said Uncle John. "That and the memory of 1857 and 1873, when everything collapsed and the less you had the less you lost."

"On the farm it's different," said Karl. "We have the land."

Uncle John looked at him.

"Look around you. Land is everywhere," he said. "No, I'm afraid that to make money, you have to play with fire. And the closer you get to it, the bigger the payoff."

"The Dutchman didn't seem to be looking for a payoff," said Karl.

"Thank goodness for such men," said Uncle John.

The next day his uncle left for the city. Karl was in charge of seeing the harvest downstream to the sawmill, then making proper financial settlement with the tribe.

But first came a task he dreaded. After all the work was done he gathered everyone together and told the men that this was to be his uncle's logging company's last harvest. There would be no more work. The men murmured, then drifted away. Only the Dutchman stayed, leaning against the side of one of the cabins, puffing his pipe.

"Where are you going to go?" Karl asked.

"Another river," he said.

"You could do anything," Karl said, "a man like you."

"A man like me," Hoekstra said. "A man like me does what a man like you tells him to do."

"I'm no different than you," said Karl.

"I hope for your sake you are wrong about that."

After finishing with the last payroll and reconciling balances, Karl set off to give the tribe its royalty payment, which he had meticulously documented with copies of the mill receipts. The trip to where the chief lived was a simple matter of mounting a naked ridgeline and following it. Long before the snows the chief's family would settle into the cabin where Karl and his uncle had worked and slept, the chief at Uncle John's desk doing whatever chiefs did.

Karl's breath came heavily in the thick air as he mounted a hill and got the village in sight. He was carrying a lot of money and wearing no sidearm, but he was not concerned. Nobody would come to this barren place to look for something worth stealing.

The village stood on the other side of the river. Karl descended and picked his way around the marshes until he reached the bank. He felt no urgency. He had nothing left to do in camp but pack up his things. The men had reveled late into the night and would be doing little today but paying for it.

He stepped into the water and pulled from his rucksack a light rod he had bought from the Dutchman. It came in two pieces, ingeniously held together with a ferrule of tooled tin, which had been joined to the shank with a varnished winding of thread. Karl withdrew from his pocket a reel of nickel steel his uncle had sent him from Chicago. He cinched it to the handle of the rod, then threaded the braided horse-hair line through the guides, doubled so that if his fingers slipped, it would not drop all the way back through. He had greased the line carefully the night before. To the end of it he had tied a length of gut and then another of silk so fine that he had to use a special knot Hoekstra had shown him.

Karl took out a small tin from his breast pocket and greased the gut and silk so they would float. Then he withdrew a wooden box. Into its lid he had carved his initials in the fanciest German script he could manage. He gently opened the box and took out a tiny tan fly that he had made of rabbit fur, feathers, and thread. His fingers, which had seemed so thick and unwieldy when he was learning the knots, now deftly whipped the filament around itself five times, then threaded the tip back through the loop until he had a connection he was confident could hold the wildest fish in the river. He pulled it tight, the hook biting into the edge of his thumb. Then he put a bit of grease on the fly itself, grooming it as carefully as he might ready himself for church.

When he was satisfied, he stripped out some line and waited, watching the water. There were tiny midges in the air, but nothing to interest a trout of any size. Karl saw no rings on the surface of the water that would have marked feeding fish like a bull's eyes. He gazed up and down along the far bank until he spotted some fallen timber lying just inside the line of bubbles in the current and parallel to it. A few days ago he would have thought to free it up and send it downriver, but now it suggested to him another purpose.

Sliding his feet along the river bottom, feeling for obstacles, he carefully pushed upstream. With folding money in his pocket he could not afford to take an accidental swim. When he stopped and looked up, he met another pair of eyes.

An Indian brave about his age stood ten yards off the bank in a thicket of reeds. Karl nodded to him. Nothing passed the young man's face.

Karl's line trailed downstream until he lifted it from the water in one smooth pull and set it down straight, cutting an angle to the current. His first cast landed well short of the submerged timber, but he was pleased with the soft presentation of the fly and the even float of leader and line. He looked up at his observer to see if he, too, appreciated the technique but received no satisfaction. Then, checking behind him to see how much leeway he had for the backcast, he slipped two more pulls from the reel, lifted the whole length of line, sending it backward, then stopped the rod abruptly. He waited a count and sent it forward again. The fly uncoiled in front of him and landed a little upstream of where he wanted it, but a quick flip mended the line and gave him the drift he needed. Sure enough, from beneath the fallen log flashed an apparition. Karl lifted the rod to set the hook and felt the desperate tug of life.

It took a few minutes to bring the wildly darting, running beast under control. Then he patiently reeled it in until, holding his rod high over his head, he could reach down and seize it by the tail.

The fish was no more than sixteen inches, but, as the Dutchman used to say, it had shoulders. A fine offering it would make when he reached the village. Perhaps, he thought, the chief would ask him to share a meal.

When he looked up, the young Indian was gone. The fish arched its back. Then came a sickening splash as it broke free of his hold.

Shortly he heard movement upstream. The young Indian stood on a raised bank above a deep, murky pool. He glanced at Karl, then set eyes on the impossibly dark waters for a long moment before lifting his arm and hurling a spear. It pierced the river with hardly a splash. The butt end rose, splashing madly this way and that. The young man took several quick, sure steps downriver, pulling in the cord attached to the spear, then plunged his arm in up to the shoulder. When he raised it again, he had a fish twice as large as the one Karl had lost. The Indian flung it unceremoniously to the bank. The brutal efficacy was like an arrow striking Karl's breast.

"Good fish," he shouted.

But by then the Indian had vanished into the reeds. Karl reeled in his line, broke down the rod, and pulled himself from the river.

When he reached the village, the chief was waiting for him. His skin had the weathered color of deadfall stripped of bark. Alongside him was the brave.

Karl showed the chief his meticulous documentation, but the chief showed no interest.

"You have the money?" he said.

"Here," Karl said, handing it to him. "Don't you even want to count it?"

"Your people are like fire," said the chief. "You cannot number the flames."

"What will you do with the money?" Karl asked.

"We will not buy sticks like yours for fishing," said the chief. The brave laughed. "My son said you lost your grayling."

"And your son caught his," Karl said.

"When we want a thing, we want it only for itself, and we get it," said the chief. "Your people always are thinking about something more."

"Like beauty and grace, you mean," said Karl.

"It is a strange time and place for you to be speaking of such things," said the chief.

More than a decade passed before Karl worked these currents again with greased line and fur and feather. By then his soul had come dangerously close, through brutal experience, to losing the very thought of grace.

5

AFTER KARL ALIGHTED FROM THE TRAIN in Chicago, he wandered the streets, duffel bag in hand, taking it all in. People wore every manner of costume, from top hats and bowlers to what Karl's father, leafing through the Sears, Roebuck catalog, called "immigrant caps."

The women all seemed larger than life, with their bustles and high, corseted busts. Karl had never seen such an acreage of exposed female skin, an effect multiplied by the number of months in which the only women he had seen were in the Indian village, as wrapped-up as their papooses. At some point in his wide-eyed meander he came upon the bright blue waters of the lake. Many women were out sunning themselves: shameless, smooth, wonderful legs below their bloomers. What a grand thing a city was!

It did not take long before Karl's own appearance began to make him self-conscious. No matter how diverse the fashion he saw on the streets, he did not run into anyone else looking like a lumberjack. His untrimmed beard itched with each young woman he caught noticing it. His utility shirt felt crude, his boots cumbersome. Suddenly he wanted refuge, so he asked directions to the address Uncle John had given him.

As he passed the Board of Trade, about which he had heard so much complaining in Abbeville, he could not help thinking of it as an enormous grain elevator, with all the green growth of the plains pouring through it. He pushed open the heavy door of the building where his uncle had his office and stepped into a limestone cave lit by hundreds of lamps. It was not in any ordinary sense a place of worship, but it had a church's solemn hush.

On either side of the lobby identical staircases rose like the ascent of angels. At the landing of what was labeled "mezzanine" the staircases gave way to more conventional steps. He climbed and climbed until, by the time he reached the floor marked 5, he was perspiring.

When he found the door with his uncle's name on it, he knocked. No answer. In Abbeville you usually just stepped into folks' houses and called out a name, but here he wasn't sure. He knocked again and heard an exasperated voice say, "Come on in, for heaven's sake!"

Inside stretched a long, empty room with a few vacant chairs and low, round tables holding newspapers in various states of disarray. He noticed a window set into the wall at the far end of the room. Behind it sat a woman with flame-red hair pulled up into a swirl.

"Didn't you hear me?" she said through a round hole in the glass.

"I thought you said to come in," he said, leaning toward retreat.

"Three times," she said. "You're all sweaty." The word in her mouth made him feel exposed. "Is the elevator broken?"

"You keep the grain right here?" he said.

She looked at him as if he were the one who used foreign words like mezzanine.

"An elevator," she said. "It rides people up and down."

"Well, I never heard of anything like that," he said.

"Where in the world do you come from?" she said.

"From Michigan just now," he said. "Been logging there. Originally from a place in farm country you never heard of."

"Then you must be Karl," she said out of nowhere. "Go sit down and cool yourself. He's been a regular pest, asking after you."

She disappeared, and moments later Uncle John entered the waiting room, looking nothing like he did in the woods. Under a starched white collar and vest flashed a silk tie stuck through with a gold pin.

"Hello, son," he said, offering his cultivated hand. "Luella? Where did you disappear to? I need you to help me get this lad into the appropriate straitjacket."

The redheaded woman emerged from the door.

"Should we try the Fair?" the young woman said.

A county fair in the middle of the city?

"Ask for Will Doyle," said Uncle John.

"What should we be looking for?" asked the young woman.

"Two good suits with waistcoats. Shirts. Ties. Everything it would take to make you look at him twice."

"I've done that already," said the young woman.

Luella. Karl rolled the word silently on his tongue. It made him tingle.

"Well?" she said, looking right at him. He could not think of a single word beyond her name. She seemed delighted to prolong his state of suspension. But finally she spoke again. "The boss has given us orders." Then she actually took his hand, as if the fiddler had started to play and the whole room was awhirl. "Come on. Don't be afraid of me. I'm just another girl."

"Don't you believe her," Uncle John warned.

The Fair turned out to be an enormous emporium. Just inside the door they passed a counter of women's lotions and elixirs that smelled so sweet he felt faint. Next came a counter with so many different kinds of handbags that he thought every woman in the city must have wanted one that was unique to her. Then it was up the stairs to a room that held enough jackets and pants to clothe all of Cobb County.

"And what may I be doing for a hearty young gentleman such as yourself this fine afternoon?" said a man even more dapper than Uncle John.

"He needs to be made presentable," said Luella.

"And who would you be proposing to present him to, Miss?" said the man. With his accent and lovely tenor voice he seemed almost to be singing. "Would it be your family, then?"

"Oh, my, no," said Luella with a little more vehemence than Karl wanted to hear. "This is the nephew of Mr. Schumpeter."

"Well, then, he could buy the whole store," said the salesman.

Karl looked around him. Nobody had enough money for that.

"I'm just a farmer and a logger," he said, "and I'm here to get an education."

"Then let's find you a suit of clothes befitting the educated man you are to become."

Karl followed the two of them to a rack that must have held fifty suits. When they reached it, the salesman took a step or two back and looked Karl up and down.

"I'd say a 40," said the salesman. "Now here is a classic." He pulled a dark-blue suit off the rod and sent the other clothes dancing. "Can you feel how smooth that is?" he asked, inviting Karl to finger the weave. Under Karl's callused fingers, the fabric might as well have been silk.

"I am under strict instructions to make sure he comes home with something with a vest," said Luella.

"Ah," said the salesman, thumbing the edge of his own. "I think Mr. Schumpeter is correct, though a waistcoat is not for everyone. It takes a certain bearing to carry it. But let's first think only of fit."

He lifted the dark suit he had taken down.

Karl reached for the hanger, but the man turned and walked away. Karl looked at Luella.

"You have to try on the pants, too, silly," she said.

Karl was still confused.

"Not right here in the middle of the floor," she said. "Just follow him."

The next hour was extraordinary. Luella chose suits and shirts for him to try on. She touched each of them all over, inspecting the weave and the stitching inside, before handing it to him so he could go into the little closet and place it, fresh from her hands, directly against his skin. Then he would come out and model for her how the shirt or suit or jacket looked on him, and sometimes she would actually touch it on him, the shoulders, the calf—even, praise God, the waist. What's more, she did not seem the least hesitant about it. What kind of incredible women did they raise here?

When they were finished shopping, Karl noticed in the mirror Luella looking at both sides of him.

"You wouldn't be reconsidering now, would you, Miss?" said the salesman.

"Reconsidering?"

"Bringing this one home."

"He does look nice, doesn't he?" she said, and Karl felt like a stallion that had taken a ribbon.

Luella signed the store ticket. Though Karl knew his uncle's generosity would pay the bill, his gratitude went to her, and he said so.

"You are a real gentleman," she said. "Do you know that? For someone raised with goats."

OVER THE NEXT SEVERAL days his uncle tutored Karl in the firm's basics.

"My company deals in promises," Uncle John explained. "Promises to sell a certain quantity of grain at a certain price on a specific date in the future. People buy and sell those promises until the day arrives. Then whoever has sold it last must fulfill the promise, either in grain or cash."

"What is the point?" said Karl.

"The only way to control the future is to pay its price today," said Uncle John.

Within a few weeks he moved Karl from the office to the Board of Trade itself.

The trading floor spread out over what seemed like an acre under high, grimy windows. Above it stood enormous clock-like devices. An attendant manned each, following the action on the floor and moving the dial's single arm, clockwise on a rising market, counterclockwise on a decline.

Karl's first job was to take orders over the leased telegraph line that connected to Uncle John's office down the street. When he received an order, Karl dispatched it via one of a half-dozen young toughs who ran them to the Schumpeter traders in the pits.

Karl was amazed at how this stone-hard city transformed grain into an abstraction, but it was not as though the physical world did not intrude. A surfeit of rain moved the market, though no one on the trading floor suffered a drop of it falling on his shoulders. A military upheaval in Europe stampeded the market, though no one here heard a cannon.

Every day as Karl walked home to the boardinghouse, he passed a little square where street-corner orators condemned everything Karl was learning how to do:

"Who are the wolves who wager on our toil?" Predators speculating upon the very food in our children's mouths. They buy and sell you as surely as slave masters. They stir great waves of panic, then mount the crests for gain.

"There is nothing in this world that is not material. Love? Religion? The milk of human kindness? Money and class crush them.

"But one day the contradictions will all lie bare before you. The workers of the world will come together in the great, inevitable surge of history. Class will battle class, and the weak shall rise up as one and bring the predators down!"

The next day Karl told Luella about the man.

"You should have seen him," he said. "He had a head of hair out to here and a beard scragglier than any I saw in the woods. And the mouth on him. He doesn't stop for a breath."

"Maybe he has a lot to say," said Luella.

Less than a week later, one of the regular traders fell seriously ill. Uncle John asked Karl if he was ready to take his place.

"You have everything in your head that you need," Uncle John said. "Now we must find out what's in your belly."

That afternoon Karl pulled at his starched collar, cleared his throat, and asked Luella to dinner. She accepted immediately, and he wondered why he had waited so long.

As afternoon wore into evening, his uncle left for some engagement or another, and the activity in the office slowed. Luella came to Karl's desk, and side by side they looked out the window into LaSalle Street. The city lay before him as if it were his. Luella on his arm, he tipped his hat to one of the clerks and winked at the doorman, who got them a carriage and received a nice gratuity for his trouble.

Karl had chosen a fancy place on the Gold Coast north of the river near where Uncle John lived—along with the Swifts and Armours and Potter Palmers and everyone else with a name. As soon as the two of them stepped into the restaurant, he realized he had made a mistake. Luella, who had always before appeared cosmopolitan in her bright white shirtwaist and black skirt, here seemed totally out of place. The preening little maître d' did not even meet her eyes as he suggested that she leave her knitted shawl at the coat check in the tone he might have used to ask her to take off a pair of shit-smeared boots.

"Are you all right?" Karl asked as they were led toward a dark, far-away corner of the restaurant.

"Why wouldn't I be?"

"We could go somewhere else."

"Only if you think we should," she said.

"I don't think any such thing," he said.

The restaurant was lighted by candles, which gave the lacy expanses of the ladies' white gowns an antique glaze. The menu came in French. He knew a few words from Abbeville, but they weren't the words that described this fare, so he had to seek the waiter's help.

"Why don't I just bring you some sort of steak," the waiter said.

"And some corn," said Karl.

"Corn," said the waiter. "Yes, of course."

When the waiter had gone, Karl arranged the napkin in his lap and surveyed the array of implements before him, which seemed extensive enough to perform surgery. Luella said nothing.

"I don't know why they say this is such a great place," he said.

"You really don't, do you," Luella said. She reached over and took his hand where it lay next to a rank of spoons. "It's because people like me don't come here."

They ate as quickly as they could and left. She gave her address to the carriage driver, who headed south and west into precincts of the city Karl had never traveled before. There were sweatshops and small restaurants and greengrocers and block upon block of three-story tenements. At some point he got a whiff of what smelled like the farm, and he wondered if they could already have reached the city's outskirts. Soon it was stronger than any farm he had ever known.

"That's the stockyards," she said. "You get used to it."

She leaned forward and tapped the driver on the shoulder.

"Here," she said.

The carriage rolled to a stop. The horse twitched. Karl jumped down onto the rutted street and came around to help her, but by the time he got there she was already on the way to the rickety steps of her flat.

"I'm sorry," Karl said.

"You didn't know," Luella said. "I should have."

Through the window of the tenement across the street somebody was shouting in a language Karl had never heard.

"Will you be all right?"

She smiled, put her hand to his cheek, and gave him the slightest, sweetest kiss on the lips.

"Next time," he said, "I'll be smarter about where we go."

"Next time," she said, "you will be smarter about who you go with."

"Don't say that," he said.

"I won't have to," she said. "Others will."

In the morning his uncle called him into his office before Karl left for the Board of Trade and his maiden descent into the pits. Karl brought with him a small notebook in which to record his uncle's instructions.

"You were with that girl Luella last night," said Uncle John.

"Yes, sir," Karl said.

"Did you have a good time?"

"She's very nice."

"Have you seen her here this morning?" said his uncle.

"I was a little worried," said Karl.

"There is no place for sentiment in business," his uncle said.

"Yes, sir."

"Do you know why you haven't seen Luella?" his uncle asked.

"No, sir."

"She has become much too familiar," said Uncle John. "I had to let her go."

"But I was the one who wanted for us to go out," said Karl. "I am the one you should blame."

"Business and sentiment, lad," said his uncle. "You must keep them scrupulously separate. When you don't, someone always gets hurt."

Karl left his uncle's office in a daze, contradictions colliding within him. An opportunity of a lifetime, brigaded by cruelty. The sweetness of the city's freedom causing injustice and suffering. As he stepped onto the sidewalk, a newspaper hawker shouted the morning's headline. Another bank had failed. The markets had been getting more and more jittery.

As soon as he reached the floor of the Board of Trade, the clamor and immediacy drove contradiction into retreat. On the trading floor everyone wore linen jackets, wheat green in color for the traders, who had numbered badges pinned to their lapels. Along the perimeter of what they called the pits the traders stood elbow to elbow in a line, like cornstalks at the edge of a field. A pit consisted of concentric risers ascending perhaps four feet on the outside and descending an equal distance toward the center. Each pit specialized in a single commodity—wheat, corn, rye, and so on—and each section was devoted to a specific month—July wheat, September corn, November rye. Every trader had his special place on the risers. Through sharp trading you might force a man into the poorhouse, but as long as he was in the pit you would never take his trading space.

Whenever a large order came in to buy or sell at whatever price the market would bear, a telegraph clerk slapped the order onto the counter, making a sharp noise like a starter's gun. A runner snatched it and raced toward the pits. Woe betide anyone who got in the way.

As Karl donned his trader's jacket and badge for the first time, the activity in the pit was so intense that at first he couldn't even locate the man who was to train him. Rumor had it that Sampson & Sons was trying to construct a corner in September corn. This meant they were buying heavily in an effort to take control of the supply and then ruthlessly drive up the price. When the price reached a peak they hoped to sell out at enormous profits.

The noise was furious. Men shouted and flung fingers into one another's faces. Karl found some daylight and moved through it. Behind him the crowd closed up again like water.

When he reached the top step, he finally spotted his man. Rather than go around and risk losing his target in the turbulence, Karl descended to the center of the maelstrom.

"Schumpeter & Co.!" he shouted. "Peter Mallory!"

His words were lost in the din.

Ducking outstretched arms, he reached the bottom. Down there the traders oriented themselves outward and upward, where the action was. As a result, the very center was empty and calm.

As he pushed upward again, the mob pushed back. Noise crashed over him.

"Well, there you are, sport," said Mallory, who immediately caught something out of the corner of his eye, and, like a fisherman seeing the ring of a trout's rise, wheeled and cast. The quarry was a fat, balding fellow ten feet away. Mallory hit his mark, set the hook, and completed the trade, recording it both on the order sheet and on a card he kept in his breast pocket.

"Picked that off at three-quarters," he said. "The market's already moved north of that."

Karl looked up at the balcony where an attendant was turning the arm of the indicator.

"You really have to be alert," Karl said.

Mallory looked past him. His arm flew up and in an instant he was writing again.

"By the time you see the market shift, it's too late," he said. "You always have to run ahead of the current."

Hour after hour Karl studied Mallory. Then at the end of the day the older man had Karl attempt a trade. But before he could consummate it, a bell sounded.

"You'll just have to wait till tomorrow to lose your virginity, sport," Mallory said. "Do you want to have a drink? Or are you a temperance man like your uncle?"

Karl did not drink, but he did not want to say so. Mallory's face had a glow that indicated he didn't mind anyone knowing how he was inclined. They went to a stand-up place around the corner where Karl saw a dozen familiar faces in the mirror behind the bar, as expressionless as the bottles.

"Those are the bulls," said Mallory. "They were counting on harvesting the fruits of their corner, but the price ended up within an eighth of where it started. They were expecting to get filthy rich, but they'll get filthy drunk instead. Sir, bring us two Pilsners. The lad here has just spent his first day dealing grain."

They had left their linen jackets behind, and Mallory in his suit looked as though he could work at the Fair. A bright yellow silk handkerchief stood out against his gray double-breasted jacket like a beacon in a gathering fog.

One beer led to another, and then a third. Karl savored the taste of the fields in it.

"Tomorrow you will make money, sport," Mallory said with an expansive wave of his hand. "Or else you will lose it."

He lifted his glass and Karl touched it with his. The beer was edgy, and the bubbles stung his nose.

"I don't have much money to lose," said Karl.

"Don't you worry about that," said Mallory. "The funds will be the firm's, and I will be there to catch it if it starts sliding through your fingers."

Later, when Karl got back to his room, he was exhausted but could not sleep. He blamed the muggy weather, what had happened to Luella, the bilious liquid backing up into his throat. At some point his head began to throb. The simple fact was that he could not wrest his mind from the swirling, addictive chaos of the trading floor.

The next day the opening bell approached, and Karl began to panic. Mallory wasn't there. When he finally did arrive, he looked more than a little ill.

"I don't imagine you went right home," said Karl.

Mallory put his hand in his pocket and pulled out a box of matches with the silhouette of a can-can dancer and the name of a club.

"I guess I went there," he said.

"What did your wife say?"

"I didn't wake her up to find out," said Mallory.

Just then a runner brought an order. Mallory nodded him toward Karl.

"As you can see," Mallory explained to the runner, "I am a mite under the weather. My understudy here will be at the tiller."

For the next several hours Karl felt as if he were fighting to keep from capsizing. At some point, though, he began to get the sense of the waters. He filled so many orders he lost count of how much corn had moved through his hands. When the closing bell sounded and the dial above the trading floor stopped moving, his whole body felt as if it might collapse.

"Well, sport," said Mallory, "by my count you've made your uncle two thousand dollars richer."

"Two thousand dollars," said Karl.

"Now let's go give ourselves a reward," said Mallory.

This time Karl came a little closer to keeping up with his mentor at the bar, goaded on by a honky-tonk piano like nothing Karl had ever heard. Mallory wanted to take Karl to another place and introduce him to some can-can dancers, but Karl had a different idea.

He got his mentor into a carriage, then hailed one for himself. He did not know Luella's address, so he offered to direct from up front.

"I've driven a lot of buggies," he confided.

"Ay," said the driver, "and I've driven a lot of drunks."

Row after row of tenements lined the street, which teemed with vendors. The clamor was like an open-air version of the corn pit, if you could call the fetid air open. He tried to focus on individual buildings, but they were all a wobbly blur.

"Slow down, please," he shouted. The driver grumbled but complied. This made Karl's eyes somewhat more useful, but still he could not tell one tenement from another.

Suddenly a gang of street urchins surrounded the carriage, forcing it to come to a stop. Hands stretched out to Karl. Cries of "Mister! Mister! Mister!" Then he felt a hand reaching into the pocket of his coat. Somehow he found the agility to seize it.

The other boys scattered. A policeman across the way cast a wary eye in the direction of the scuffle, as if to determine who was assaulting whom. The boy wriggled and twisted, but Karl's hand had not lost the strength of the forest.

"I'll turn you over to that officer there," he said, which set the boy off again. "Unless you can help me, that is."

"Shit on that," said the boy. "I don't do the nasty for nobody."

"Show me where Luella Grundy lives and I'll let you go," said Karl.

The boy looked at Karl with all the city's dangerous knowledge in his twelve-year-old eyes.

"Gimme a nickel?" he said.

"If you stick with me until I see her," Karl said.

"Hey, nothin' doin'," said the boy. "What if she ain't there?"

"So what'll it be, lad?" said Karl. "Me or the law?"

The boy squirmed again for a moment, then stopped. Karl helped him into the carriage.

"Where to now, mister?" said the driver.

"Wherever the boy says," said Karl.

"Two blocks down, then a block north," said the boy.

The driver snapped the horse into action. The policeman watched them pass—man and boy—and shook his head.

When they reached the place, Karl half recognized it, but in his present state he wasn't sure. He held out the nickel to draw the boy up the front steps and into the vestibule.

"This is the difference in the price of a bushel I bought this morning and the one I sold this afternoon," he said. The boy looked at him as if he were speaking in tongues.

Luella's full name was on one of the doors. He had expected to see her father's. He knocked, heard footsteps, then the door swung open.

"Here," he said to the boy and flipped a coin into the air. The boy snatched it at the top of its arc and bolted. It was not his fault that Luella was already closing the door.

"Please," Karl said. "Hear what I have to say."

He found himself speaking to a single eye.

"I had no idea this was going to happen to you," he said. "I tried to talk to him, but he wouldn't listen. I'm a farm boy. I don't know about these things. All I do know is that you were kind to me. And that I liked you. And that I was lonely. And that it seemed possible you were, too."

She came into the hall with him, closing the door partway behind her until her back braced against it.

"I'm not mad at you," she said.

"What will you do?"

"Find another job. I have skills, you know."

He wasn't exactly sure just now what he knew and what he didn't.

"I'm afraid that I have had something to drink," he confessed.

"I can see that," she said.

"I was in the pit today," he said. "Trading. I made a lot of money."

"That's what people do there," she said. "It's a very selfish place. Everybody doing things only for themselves."

She looked at him in a way that made him feel he was losing her.

"You do something for me, Luella," he said.

"And you know how to flatter a girl," she said. "Did you learn that on that farm of yours?"

"I don't want to be a farmer," he said.

She looked at him strangely, almost sad. Then she turned.

"Wait," he said. "What did I do?"

"One day and the money already has you," she said.

"It isn't like that," he said. "Here, take it. I don't care about the money."

He lifted her hand and turned it palm up so he could empty his pocket into it. There was enough for her to live on for weeks.

"What is this for?" she asked.

"For what happened to you," he said, closing her hand on the bills.

She turned again and opened the big old door.

"Please don't think ill of me," he said.

"Are you going to come in or not?" she said, stepping back to make way for him. Behind her was a single room with a couch and bureau and neatly made bed.

"Where are your parents?" he said.

"I've been on my own since I was fifteen," she said.

"Are you sure it is all right?" he said from the doorway.

"It will be just fine," she said.

6

EMIL SCHUMPETER WAS NOT A LETTER writer. About the only time he felt the need was to offer condolences upon someone's passing or to scold Sears, Roebuck. Then he would spend countless hours worrying the language, which never seemed less like his first than when he dipped his pen into the black void of an inkwell. It took a lot to get Emil to confront that abyss.

So when Karl found on his bed a letter in his father's Saxon hand, he broke the seal with trembling fingers. But instead of heralding death or illness or telling him to come home, it announced that Cristina Vogel had left for Chicago to spend the summer as a seamstress, staying with her mother's sister, who had escaped Abbeville at nineteen to marry a man more than half again her age. His father thoughtfully included the address.

The news was welcome, but not without complication, coming as closely as it did upon Karl's evening at Luella's flat. And oh, what an extraordinary evening it had been. Luella had been more openly affectionate with him than anyone in Abbeville would have dared. When they'd parted, disheveled, Luella had thanked him for having more discipline than she. Still, things had happened under her caresses that before had only happened to him in dreams. He said he would, of course, do the honorable thing. She seemed to find that amusing and sent him on his way.

After receiving the letter Karl went directly to the place where Cristina was staying. The man who answered his knock wore a white dress shirt without its collar and a pair of bright red silk suspenders that secured his pants loosely over his belly like a cartoon barrel around a poor man's middle.

"No solicitors," the man said.

"I've come to call on Cristina Vogel," Karl said.

"Oh, you have, have you? I don't wonder that she already has begun to attract the bees. Unfortunately, you will have to fly honeyless back to your hive."

"I'm Karl Schumpeter," he said. "Cristina and I knew each other in Abbeville."

"Well," said the portly man, "that is another matter entirely."

It was not at all clear whether he meant entirely better or entirely worse.

"We were friends," said Karl. "I think she would tell you that."

"If you are friends," said the portly man, "then you must know that she is engaged to be married."

All Karl was able to manage was a whisper.

"I have been away."

"Engaged to Harley Ansel," said the portly man.

Harley Ansel. How could she promise herself to Harley Ansel?

"You seem stricken, young man," the man with suspenders said. "Why don't you come in? I'll get you some water. Cristina is in her room."

"Maybe I'd better just go," said Karl.

"If she wants to say hello to you," the man with suspenders said, "I see no reason why she should not."

Harley Ansel. Karl had misjudged her, misjudged the reason she had ventured to Chicago, too, pathetically misjudged that.

Cristina entered the room.

"You came," she said.

"I just heard," he said.

"I hoped that you would."

"So you wouldn't have to tell me yourself," he said.

"Hoped that you would . . . come," she said.

She was dressed more stylishly than he had ever seen her. A woman like this could live in the world Karl was now exploring as gracefully as she had in the one they had both left. But it was not to be with him.

"My father wrote me," he said.

"Yes," she said. "I asked him to."

"But he didn't say anything about Harley Ansel."

Karl tried not to let the name sound bitter, but he could taste it.

"Your father doesn't know," she said, sitting down in a big, over-stuffed chair. Karl seated himself across from her. "I told my parents that if they said a word before I was ready, I would never return home."

"Ready?"

"I needed," she said, "this one last chance."

Karl sat back.

"Chance," he said.

She lowered her eyes to her lap.

"Do you hate me for it?" she said.

"I didn't even know you liked Harley Ansel," he said. Then he stopped himself. There was no point doing this to her.

"I didn't like him," she said. "Don't."

"Well, you sure enough found an odd way to express it," Karl blurted out.

This time she did not avoid his eyes. She stood right up to them.

"I do not want to marry someone simply because my father thinks well of his prospects," she said.

Her hands lay crossed in her lap. Karl stood and went to the window, which was hung with brocade. His hand upon the curtain stirred a mote of dust.

"I have felt the same," he said, "not wanting the life I have waiting for me back in Abbeville."

"I came to Chicago because I needed to find out what my own prospects are," she said.

"You want to be a seamstress?" Karl said.

"What is it that you want, Karl?" she said.

He stuffed his hands into his pockets, looked downward again, put his toe into the carpet as if it were loam.

"What I can't have," he said.

"Maybe you're giving up too easily," she said.

"I've gotten a taste of certain things here," he said.

"Well, then, let's stay."

He was sure she didn't really mean to speak of them as an "us."

"But at the same time I have felt the pull of home," he said. "Frankly, Cristina, you have been a big part of that."

There, he had said it.

"If you do go back, you should bring with you the things from here that you have come to love," she said.

"And what about you?" he said.

"You could bring me, if you wanted," she said.

On the street outside the window an ice cart was clop-clopping up the stone. A dog poked his nose against the arm of a boy seated on a stoop. A woman across the way was shaking a tablecloth out an upstairs window.

"I would try," he said, "if you weren't spoken for."

"I came here to find out whether I had any chance of avoiding being pushed into a terrible mistake," she said.

"What do we do?" he said.

"I guess we should take some time and find out," she said.

For the next several months Karl spent his days in the chaos of the pit just waiting for the moment he could leave and call on Cristina at her aunt's. Sometimes they stepped out for dinner, and he could barely control the surge of feeling he had with her on his arm. On a number of occasions they visited the sprawling white World's Columbian Exposition on the lakefront and witnessed all the marvels of the globe and the colonnaded promise of the future.

It took weeks before they dared to embrace. Then weeks more before she offered her lips. Even then she did not open them as Luella had.

At some point Karl felt compelled to tell Uncle John what was happening.

"We don't want to go back and work the farm," Karl said.

"There are other ways," Uncle John said.

"Abbeville is so small," said Karl.

"In the center of a very large world," said his uncle, "and increasingly connected to it. Today the train and telegraph. Tomorrow, who can know? But whatever develops will offer opportunity, opportunity that a man of promise such as yourself is uniquely prepared to seize. Become large in a small place, and eventually you can make the world come to you."

"But things are so tough right now," said Karl. "Businesses going under. Banks failing."

"The very time to be bold," said Uncle John.

Over the next several days the two of them studied large books at the Board of Trade that showed patterns of membership. As Karl's uncle had suspected, Abbeville was a niche waiting to be filled.

With Uncle John's financial backing Karl got a place on the Board of Trade. Karl signed a contract that bound him to a relationship with Schumpeter & Co. for ten years, during which time he would pay off the loan. Karl's board seat would allow him to avoid the gouging price every Chicago elevator and trading firm extracted, so even with loans to pay, he could make a decent income for himself and still do better for his neighbors than any of the competition.

Next he planned the construction of a modern grain elevator. Abbeville's farmers had to take their crops either to Simon Prideaux, the Frenchest of the French, or to distant locations, which cost them precious time and forced them to deal with strangers. The construction of a new facility would be costly, of course, but land was readily available along the railroad, and any bank would see that Karl's proposition was nothing short of inevitable.

Uncle John took Karl to his own personal banker to do the deal. It was a simple mortgage, structured so that no money moved until Karl needed it and thus no unnecessary interest accrued. At his uncle's suggestion Karl made the instrument out to cover another property upon which he had secured an option. This was to be the location of a grand new home across the tracks from the elevator.

"Be careful, Karl," Cristina said.

"Don't worry," he said.

"I mean thinking it is easy," she said. "You have fought a horse and plow. You know the kind of effort this money is based on, the seasons of disappointment."

They were walking at the lakeshore. A light breeze kept them cool under the sun of a perfect day. It also blew the city smells back inland so that, as they looked outward, to all their senses they might have been five hundred miles from anywhere.

"I think it is time," he said.

"I'm afraid to ask for what," she said.

"To go home," he said, "together."

She stopped and faced him.

"Are you asking me to marry you, Karl Schumpeter?" she said.

"I know you are promised to someone else," he said, afraid now to look at her.

"I am promising myself to you now," she said.

"What about Harley Ansel?"

"He already knows," she said.

Then she kissed him the way Luella had. Before God she did.

They wed in the church next to her aunt's flat, honeymooned at a hotel near the Auditorium, where they went to a concert. They also took in the majestic Columbian Exposition one last time. Karl wanted another look at the machine that fired the lights so bright that they said the man in the moon could see them.

Before leaving for Abbeville, he entrusted to Uncle John the funds he had accumulated in the pit.

"I will treat your money as if it were my own," Uncle John said. "By the way, have you had any further contact with that girl who worked here? What was her name?"

"I wrote her," said Karl. "She didn't reply."

Strictly speaking, this was true. He was afraid to tell him anything more.

"Good," said Uncle John.

7

BY THE TIME KARL AND CRISTINA RE-
turned to Abbeville, the tough economy was
beginning to ease. The price of corn rose, and Karl was ready to capi-
talize on it. Just as Uncle John had said, the moment to be bold had
been when everyone thought you were a fool to dare.

Foremost among Karl's doubters was his father.

"They say you are building a monument to yourself along the right-
of-way," he said, "and a palace to go along with it."

"One day that elevator will overflow," Karl said.

"And the house with all the rooms?" his father said.

"That, too," Karl smiled.

His father rose from his desk, using tightly clenched fists to push
himself up. It was the first time Karl had ever noticed the wear of time
on him.

"Have you seen Harley Ansel?" Karl's father asked.

"He hasn't been to town since Cristina and I came home," Karl
said.

"I imagined he is pleased to see you so far in debt," said his father.

"Debt creates wealth," said Karl. "That is what your brother taught me."

"Brothers," said his father.

"I have seen it work," said Karl.

"You have seen it," said his father.

"Look at how successful he is," said Karl.

His father glared at him as if Karl had just broken a perfectly good plow on a rock.

"Be careful of Harley Ansel," his father said. "He has not been pining away for loss of love. He has been bettering himself. He will go to Urbana in the fall. He plans to become a lawyer."

"Good for him," said Karl. "When he returns, maybe I will send some business his way."

"It won't be business that he'll want from you," said Karl's father.

EVERY DAY KARL and Cristina visited the site of their new house, which Cristina had dubbed the "Karlesium." First came the hole, then the skeleton, then the skin. One particular morning as the project neared completion, Cristina went to check on the summer kitchen and Karl squatted down to watch a colony of ants that had established itself next to the front walk. The insects bustled in and out of the hill, industrious but seemingly without a purpose, like the men in the pits. So must all of our activity look to the eye of God, Karl thought. And He must want it this way, since He rewards it so richly.

"Those little critters get their building done a little faster than you do," said a voice behind him.

When Karl had left Abbeville, Fritz had still been singing alto in the children's choir. Now he possessed a basso as big as the pedal tones on the church organ and stood taller than Karl by almost a head. He had also become a bit of a dandy. A boater sat atop his head at a jaunty angle, and he had clad himself in a silk vest, despite the sun.

"Henry said you put in copper wire for electric candles," he said. "I suppose it'll be electric horses next."

Karl stepped onto the porch and then into the house, which still lacked a front door.

"I'll show you," he said, leading the way to the one wall that still stood open to the studs. With his hand he felt the timbers until he found the rubber-encased wire where it went through the beam in a ceramic tube.

"Here," he said.

Fritz put out his hand hesitantly.

"There's no electricity yet," said Karl, "but eventually Samuel Insull's reach will extend to Abbeville, and then there will be enough to light every room in the house."

"You can only be in one room at a time," said Fritz.

"He makes the electricity out of moving water," said Karl.

"If he can do that," said Fritz, "maybe he can turn the shit on my soles into gold."

Karl looked down and saw a fresh shine.

"You already look like a thousand bucks, little brother," Karl said and gave Fritz a fraternal shove.

Fritz shoved back with greater force. Karl saw it coming, and braced himself. And yet he was not ready for the fierce honesty of it. He regained his balance and prepared to return the stroke. Cristina reappeared.

"What are you children up to?" she said.

WHEN THE NEW GRAIN elevator was finished, German farmers began pulling their business out of Simon Prideaux's. Karl's main competitive advantages were his membership on the Board of Trade and the telegraph line that linked him to the floor. Corn quotes came over it at the same moment they reached Uncle John's office. For the farmers of Abbeville this dulled the blades of the speculators' scythes. When the work in the fields was done, the men would gather in the steamy little plank-floored office at the elevator. Karl had a chalkboard behind his maple desk. Whenever he heard something important in the dots and dashes, he would swivel in his chair and post a number.

"The prices bob around so," said Fred Krull. "How can a man know he's being treated square?"

"Trust me," said Karl. Increasingly, they did.

A horse team inside the elevator turned a wheel that lifted the grain high into the air, where it went into a chute that led to a great common bin. In Prideaux's elevator, each farmer had a separate bin dedicated to his grain. To sell, he had to ship the grain to an elevator in Chicago, which charged gouging prices to house it until brokers in cahoots with the elevator finally sold it. When a farmer went to Karl's elevator, he received a negotiable receipt for his grain, which was not segregated from other farmers'. Sales were made on the telegraph, the receipts went out by mail, and transactions were consummated before the grain was shipped. The cost of storage in Chicago fell on the buyer.

Trains chugged up, bisected themselves, attached the full rail cars, and left empty ones in their place. Gravity pulled the work of Abbeville's hands down the chutes and into them, ready to go off to the world beyond. Then winter came and the men retired warm to their farmhouses, as confident as anyone could be who lived close to the forces that relentlessly turned life into death and death into life again.

Meanwhile, Simon Prideaux's elevator went gray in the cold sun for lack of paint. He told his customers they should beware of Karl's fancy ways. He is German, Prideaux said. He'll take and take and take.

Karl did not let this bother him. He tapped at the telegraph key, and everything tame in the world fell away, just as it had when he had stared past his rod at his fly bobbing down a bubble line.

He was taking on a good deal of risk, but he liked the financial return that debt leverage gave him. You invested a dollar of your own and borrowed four more. If the investment returned 7 percent in a year, that was thirty-five cents on your dollar, minus the bank's interest of, say, 5 percent on four dollars, or twenty cents, which left fifteen cents on your dollar, more than three times what banks paid. Of course if the investment lost 7 percent, you were out fifty-five cents of your original dollar. But nothing lost money these days.

He put down bets on land whenever anyone died without heirs. He put money into Uncle John's hands to buy stocks and corporate bonds. He started up a general store and then a farm implement business on Abbeville's main street along the tracks. Anyone could have done it, but no one else had the nerve. In time Karl's interests became so varied that hardly a freight train passed that did not stop to drop something off for him.

As his level of debt rose, so did his attention to the business of banking. Every payment he made gave some financial institution money it could lend to someone else at a profit. Karl began to think about starting a bank himself.

"I believe I'd always be worried about robbers," said Cristina.

"You don't hang on to the customers' deposits," he said. "You lend the money right back out again."

"Lending people money is a recipe for hard feelings," she said.

"When you take in deposits, it's a liability," Karl explained. "When you make a loan, it's an asset."

"It all sounds backward to me," said Cristina, drying her hands on a dish towel at the sink. "I think you'd better be cautious."

But it had gotten to the point where you just could not afford to be.

Even the farmers were getting bolder, which made a solid market for Karl's new bank. Using the new implements Karl was selling on his lot on Main Street, a man could triple the amount of land he could handle. In fact, he pretty much had to because of the equipment's cost.

As George Loeb put it in a note accompanying one of his loan payments, "They should call these infernal things John Dear."

At first the farmers had been wary of the internal combustion engine, especially when Karl brought home a Model T from Kankakee that spooked every horse in Cobb County. Soon, though, the advantages of the new type of horsepower became obvious to everyone.

This created the opportunity to break free of farming that Fritz had been looking for. Building roads would allow him to leave his mark upon the land that had left its mark on him. He wanted to make money. He wanted to have things.

"I need a stake, brother," Fritz said.

"Come around to the bank and we'll talk about it," said Karl.

Fritz was no worse a risk than half the men Karl bankrolled, and with the economy growing the way it was and the Model T catching on, somebody was going to make money paving the way to the future. It might as well be Fritz.

8

THE MORE KARL PROSPERED, THE MORE HE wanted to accomplish. Once the bank got rolling, he ran for sheriff, promising to serve for a dollar a year. In his first months in office he managed both to tame the ruffians who sometimes disturbed the peace on Saturday nights and to make the gypsies understand that when they came he was watching. But even in vigilance he sparked with energy and dreams of what Abbeville could become.

The farmers were thriving. Every train from Chicago brought new evidence of what urbanity offered—fine crystal from Tiffany, stylish Sunday clothes for the ladies, painted ceramics like beautiful shells washed in on the tide. The richest of these went to Karl and Cristina's home, and Karl never felt the need to apologize because it was the way of today's world for the man who takes the risk to get the reward. But something was missing. The future, Karl thought, needed some grander expression.

Then the idea came to him. At the Columbian Exposition, he had seen displays from every corner of the earth—sculptures, dioramas, tapestries, exotic animals in cages. On the Midway rose Ferris's great wheel. Near it were men and women in costumes from every clime, some barely wearing anything at all. But the most amazing spectacle was what made the whole white world glow: a huge, humming dynamo of copper and iron. In bulk it was to the average farm implement as the Chicago Auditorium was to the Abbeville Coliseum. But size was the least of its wonders. It performed alchemy, turning black coal into bright white light, and all you heard was a rotor humming like a celestial choir.

One day in the sixth year after Karl and Cristina had returned to Abbeville, a southbound train made a whistle stop. From it emerged a dapper man with a tiny mustache, a bright red silk handkerchief puffing up in his pocket, and a leather valise that seemed almost as big as he was. He stepped down carefully, checking the ground before alighting. It was obvious that his fancy boots had never met the leavings of a horse.

Karl and Cristina crossed the gravel road and waded heedlessly through the high grass. The little man stood on the edge of it as the train pulled away, looking into the windswept prairie waves as if they were a cold, dark sea.

"Jonathan Pryor," he said when they reached him.

"We'll just follow this little path," Karl said. "Cristina will show the way. Can I take your bag?'

"Absolutely not," said Mr. Pryor.

It did not help when Karl pulled up a carriage to avoid the walk back across the prairie and the horse immediately unloaded. Mr. Pryor did not say a thing. He just put his fancy red handkerchief to his nose.

When they got home, Cristina established him in the big room upstairs. He seemed content, but Cristina whispered to Karl out of his hearing, "I'm a little worried about the chamber pot."

That evening she put out a spread—roast beef, fresh corn, of course, and mashed potatoes. Mr. Pryor looked as though all of this was much more than he was used to, but he rose to it. By the time the evening wound down, he sat in the front parlor with the bottom buttons of his waistcoat undone and a fastidiously cut cigar between his tiny fingers.

"We need to settle on size," he said. "Machines, like people, exist with a multitude of dimensions. But with machines size is directly related to capability."

Karl was not a big man either, so he laughed easily.

"The decision will turn on how much you can afford, and this will tell us the peak load you will be able to put on the system," Mr. Pryor went on.

"Say we wanted to power the whole town," Karl said.

"How many homes and businesses?" asked Mr. Pryor.

"Say twenty-five," said Karl, "not counting the outlying farms."

"Transmission over distances is very costly," said Mr. Pryor. "Is there anything unusual in any of the businesses?"

Karl leaned forward.

"Other than the elevator," he said, "there is my general store, my implement lot with a little shack on it, the Coliseum, and a blacksmith shop that is beginning to provide fuel and repairs for horseless carriages."

"A fine invention that," said Mr. Pryor.

"And, of course, my bank," said Karl.

"You seem to be a regular Samuel Insull among the rustics," said Mr. Pryor.

"We mustn't forget the church," said Karl. "I have always worried about the candles."

"Don't tell me you care for Abbeville's souls, too," said Mr. Pryor.

The next day the engineer inspected the elevator, making a wide berth around the horses, then did some calculations on a pad of paper. As soon as he returned it to his valise, he shook Karl's hand and picked his way back to the tracks. Within minutes they heard the northbound train.

When the estimates came back by mail, they showed that lighting the whole town would be prohibitively expensive.

"I'm sorry," said Cristina.

"This is why you run the numbers," said Karl. "They tell you the future."

"The future is so lonely," said Cristina.

For all the bounty that had come their way, this part of their dream had failed them. The large house contained no sound of children. It was not for want of trying. Karl went to Cristina's bed regularly. At first they tasted ecstasy and the joyful promise of the family to which it would lead, but over time this eroded into blank and fruitless effort. Every month Cristina's blood flowed.

"There is an alternative to wiring everyone's house," Karl went on, because talking about the painful thing only made tears flow, too. "We'll install electric streetlamps. No more tripping and falling on the way home from the Coliseum. And if someone gets rowdy outside, they will be able to see my sheriff's star."

"Less schnapps would work just as well," said Cristina.

"No more stepping in puddles," Karl said.

"We don't even have gaslights, Karl."

"It will be quite an improvement, all right."

He went to Fritz to propose that he undertake the construction of the engine house.

"You will be working with Mr. Pryor," said Karl. "He will be the general contractor."

"That prissy little fellow?" said Fritz. "What will people think if they see me taking orders from him?"

"The machine will be so astounding that just being near it will make you seem a magician."

"I guess it would be a feather in my cap," said Fritz. Karl looked at his jaunty bowler. With a feather in it, he would look like an Indian chief.

"You'd better keep your head from getting too big for the cap," said Karl, "before decking it out in feathers."

Based on the initial drawings, Fritz brought in an excavation team to dig the footings. Karl thought it might be better to wait until the project settled a little more, but Fritz wanted to get a jump on the weather, so he put together a crew.

Fortunately, the weather got a jump on them, preventing the excavation for several weeks, during which time the drawings changed substantially, which would have required the original hole to have been filled and redug.

"We're a little over budget," Fritz explained, "due to the idle days of my crew. I don't know why that little fellow didn't get the scale right the first time."

"Live and learn," said Karl.

After the first misstep, Fritz refused to begin digging until he received a final set of drawings, even after Mr. Pryor assured him by telegraph that the foundation dimensions would not change. The final drawings arrived on the very same freight that delivered the great machine, crated against human curiosity in a wooden box as big as a hay wagon and the horses to pull it. Tight as it was against peering eyes, it was not waterproof, so Karl had to have Fritz protect it from the rain by rigging up huge tarps pegged down at the edges like a circus tent. When Mr. Pryor and his crew arrived, the footings were not half done, so the costs mounted again.

Karl and Cristina turned their back parlor into a dormitory, where one of the workers enjoyed pounding out ragtime on the big upright piano Cristina had ordered from the city for little fingers to play. The racy music reminded Karl of the tavern where Pete Mallory had taken him after his first day in the pit. It reminded him of Luella. He broke out the cigars and schnapps.

Night after night passed this way. Cristina soon began to resent the conversation that kept her awake in her bedroom on the first floor, sometimes even after Karl had finally repaired to his own bed in the adjoining room. There was no question of sleeping together with the men so near, and you could not make a baby in separate beds.

To speed things up, Karl persuaded Fritz to take on Samuel Scott from Martindale as his construction superintendent. Scott had been in the business for many years but had backed away as the jobs grew bigger and the need for capital increased.

"He is averse to risk," Karl explained to Fritz, "but not to hard work."

Karl saw the improvement immediately. But whenever Karl would ask how things were going, Scott would just say, "Getting there. Getting there."

Fritz, of course, told a different story. One day it would be that Mr. Pryor had made another change. The next it would be that Scott was slowing things down by always insisting on things being done in a certain way.

It seemed to take forever, but finally the project was complete. Karl called a meeting at the Coliseum.

"Come on in, everyone," he said as the farmers and townsfolk gathered in the shadows outside the door. "Plenty of seats up front."

There was a slight murmur as they moved into the sepia, kerosene-lighted hall. Karl saw Fred Krull's red face appear in the doorway. The crowd hushed as Harley Ansel walked down the aisle toward Karl.

He was back from Urbana and almost finished with his apprenticeship in a law office in Potawatomi, the county seat. They said he planned to run for Cobb County prosecutor once he had established himself in private practice. Karl and he had exchanged greetings once or twice, but they generally stayed out of each other's way. Ansel's face had no use for bygones. Karl's did not expect forgiveness, or need it.

If apologies were due, they should have come from Ansel. In the midst of the project Fritz had complained that Ansel had told him Karl was making him a laughingstock by forcing Scott on him, that everyone in Abbeville could see that Karl had no respect for him, that Karl was taking every good business opportunity for himself, then throwing Fritz the scraps. He made fun of the way Fritz dressed, said he looked like a rooster. "A rooster that can't find the chicken coop," he said.

"I told him I'm just waiting for the right woman," Fritz told Karl. "And he said, 'Better watch out or your brother will take her, too.'"

Karl advised Fritz not to pay Ansel any mind, but this was not Fritz's way. Instead he tried to ingratiate himself with the man, flattering him in public, giving him legal business from his road construction company. He would have had him do the contract for the dynamo building if Karl hadn't talked him out of it.

As the crowd in the Coliseum watched, Ansel stepped close to Karl but did not accept his hand.

"Hello, Harley," Karl said. "I didn't expect to see you here. I heard you were in Potawatomi."

"Where I live is none of your concern," said Ansel.

"There are plenty of seats," Karl said.

The murmuring in the room commenced again as more and more townsfolk and farmers filed in. Karl went to the door to see how many more were on the way. There was no moon, so it was difficult to see very far. Karl smiled.

Henry Mueller stuck out his hand when he entered with young Henry Jr. in tow.

"Hello, gents," Karl said as they shook hands.

"'Lo," said Henry Sr.

Cristina's brothers came next, finding chairs in the next-to-last row.

"What in thunder did you drag us all here for, Karl?" Will Trague's voice boomed out as if he were calling hogs.

"I'll tell you once everyone is seated," Karl said.

There was only a little grumbling.

The rows were filling up quickly. There was George Latour and, remarkably, Simon Prideaux. Behind them came a half-a-dozen of the French. This was good. What Karl brought to Abbeville, he brought for all.

As soon as everyone was seated, Karl looked over toward the elevator, where a red train lantern glowed near the engine house. He took one of the kerosene lamps off its shelf and moved it in an arc in the window. Once, twice. Then a red lantern in the invisible hand of one of Mr. Pryor's men swung twice in response.

Karl put the kerosene lamp back and went to the front of the room.

"Gentlemen," he said as the rustle subsided, "you have all noticed that my brother has been doing a little building."

"He's been doing damned little of it himself," said Ansel, which set off a flutter of laughter.

"What we've been working on will save time unloading at the elevator," said Karl, "and the faster we can move you through, the less money and trouble it costs us."

"You talking about taking on more farmers?" asked Will Hoenig.

"There's still quite a few French north of us who cart their harvest all the way to Versailles," said Karl. He pronounced it Ver-SAILS, the way everybody did. Karl made no mention of Prideaux's French customers to the south. "The more business Abbeville does, the better it is for everyone."

"The better for you," Ansel said, touching off the glottal laughter of the French.

Karl went to the window, picked up the kerosene lamp again, and moved it back and forth three times before replacing it on the ledge. Shortly thereafter came a sound that drew everyone's ear. Some pulled out their pocket watches in confusion, though it really sounded nothing like a train. Then, above the sound of the steam turbine, rose a high-pitched whir, the like of which none of the men facing Karl, save Mr. Pryor, had ever heard. Brows furrowed. Wind through a loose board in the barn? The cry of a wounded animal? Nothing in nature could make quite such a sound because nothing in nature rotated as fast upon itself as the flywheel of the dynamo, except perhaps a heavenly orb.

As the tone ascended, it gave the illusion of approach, like the rise of a train whistle. Karl thought he could actually hear the future racing toward them.

Some men fidgeted. A strange glow began to rise behind Karl like the dawn. It flickered. The men blinked.

"Well, I'll be damned," someone said.

"Can you beat that," said another.

"So that's what you was doing, you old fox."

The electric bulbs, which had been resting cold and unnoticed before three sconces, now beamed an even, golden hue.

"Gentlemen," Karl said, "I bring you light."

"Ain't it dangerous?" asked Georges Chartiens.

"No more than a mule," said Karl. "It won't kick you unless you approach it wrong."

"I heard tell of some trouble," said Simon Prideaux.

"People burning up," said Ansel. "There'll be liability there."

"Hell," said old Henry Mueller, "a lantern'll burn you if you knock it over."

Mr. Pryor stepped forward as the crowd began to break down into muttering knots.

"You are right to be concerned," he said. "Without due care, what warms can burn. What creates can also destroy."

"Amen," said George Loeb.

The farmers laughed.

"We'll leave that to the Rev. Johann here," said Karl. "The fact is, the dynamo will drive the elevator. It will light the Coliseum. It will exalt the church. It will show our way home at night. Tomorrow we begin installing streetlights."

"Next you're going to say you can make it rain," said Prideaux.

"It isn't natural," said Ansel.

There were a few agreeing grunts.

"It's as natural as lightning," Karl said. "And like a spring storm, it will bring increase. This is only the beginning, gentlemen. Together we will build Abbeville strong."

"You running for office again, Karl?" said Fred Krull.

"It's just that we've got to defend ourselves," said Karl.

"Haven't you heard?" said Ansel. "The Injuns are all dead."

"They got chased straight off the plains, didn't they," said Karl. "And do you know why?"

"Because they didn't have dynamos?" sneered Prideaux.

"Because they wouldn't change," said Karl.

Mr. Pryor did not run a line to Karl and Cristina's house until the elevator was operating completely under artificial power, the church was aglow, and the streetlights had done their magic. By the time

Karl's house lit up, nobody said a thing about it, except Fritz, who thought Karl should have included his house, too, even though he was unwilling to put in the wiring to take advantage of it.

The streetlights turned out to be a form of entertainment. Often farmers would bring their wagons and teams into town at dusk. The sun would set, the lights would come on, and they would haul out the *Chicago Tribune* and read it in the middle of the street, just because they could. Only at the Coliseum was opinion mixed, as young folks now had even more trouble eluding the eyes of their elders.

Except on days when there were square dances, the dynamo only operated from 6 A.M. until 9 P.M., when every self-respecting person was in bed. Each night at that hour Karl left his house, walked across the prairie, stepped over the tracks, and entered the engine house to disengage the clutch, close down the big valves, and bank the coal fire. The lights on the street would flicker and die. The windows of the Schumpeter house would darken. And then there would be silence—and for Karl, a feeling of things still to be done.

After turning out the electricity Karl always made one last check of the bank, lighting a kerosene lamp with a kitchen match as he entered. The building had only one room, apart from the vault, which was in effect a separate structure at the rear. A single large table dominated the center of the room. On it men laid their hats when they came to Karl asking for a little help. The tabletop was always strewn with papers—reports from the Board of Trade, new state banking regulations, flyers from implement manufacturers.

Fritz also used the bank as his office, so on one wall hung charts showing the cost of various building materials and pictures of the big road-building implements for which Fritz had acquired a capital-intensive taste.

This was of no direct concern to the Schumpeter Bros. partnership, which had come into being when painters put the big black letters across the whitewashed wall of the elevator. There was no formal agreement between Karl and Fritz. Karl simply grew tired of Fritz's complaints and cut him in on the elevator, general store, and implement lot, though he never let him into the business of the bank, which would have required the approval of state banking authorities. Fritz for parity kept the paving business for himself.

When Karl divided the partnership income each month, he invested most of his share with Uncle John. Fritz spent his as soon as he got it, then started asking for advances. There was no mystery why. Fritz had finally taken a bride. Or, as Cristina said, had been taken.

Karl rarely brooded over any of this. But sometimes, late at night, after he returned to the silent house, he would sit at the kitchen table totting up the day's numbers and thinking about the action in the pits, the way the prices rose after they fell and fell after they rose, how the seasons came and went and Cristina's blood flowed every four weeks, and with it the sadness. Then he would snuff out the oily flame of the lamp and go to bed to wait for the morning.

9

WHEN I RETURNED FROM THE CEME-
tery to the house Grampa had built, it
was still early. I had bought some food on the way down from Chicago
so I wouldn't have to go chasing all over Cobb County for my dinner.
As I went inside I heard the birds in the trees and remembered the
summers of my boyhood, when we would spend weeks in Abbeville.
Every morning I woke up to the mourning doves. With nobody my
age to play with, I was sure they were mourning me.

I was in just such a mood one day when the flicker of spinning
blades outside scared the birds silent. It was Grampa pushing the
mower over the sparse lawn in front of the house. Strictly speaking, he
could have let it go. In farm country nobody admired or criticized another on the basis of a crop you did not harvest. But Grampa was out
there with his hand mower once a week anyway, as if for sport.

I swung my feet over the edge of the high bed and slid down until
they touched the cool wood of the floor. My heel encountered something hard and icy. It was the milk-glass chamber pot that Grandma
placed there during our visits for my convenience during the night. It

was true that it was easier to kneel down and relieve myself into it than to grope my way downstairs in the dark. But in the morning the thing mortified me, especially having to carry it past everyone to the bathroom, the yeasty smell coming up like shame. With my heel I pushed the pot farther back under the bed.

I dressed and went downstairs empty-handed. Grandma was moving about the kitchen—having heard me stirring above her—putting Butternut slices into the old chrome toaster that only did one side at a time, retrieving a box of cereal from the pantry, pouring juice and milk.

I sat down at the table where a plate of white-frosted cinnamon rolls lay on the shiny oilcloth table covering. I tore a chunk off one of the rolls and let it sweeten my morning.

"You can sit down, Grandma," I said. "I'll take care of myself."

"If I sit down too much, I'll rust," she said.

I grabbed a spoon out of the drawer and a paper napkin from a tin holder decorated with engravings of the World's Columbian Exposition of 1893. Then I wolfed down a bowl of brightly colored Kix and drained the pastel milk. I was done just as Grandma finished buttering the toast, which I snatched as I scooted out of the room.

"Mind the crumbs," Grandma called.

I bounded up the stairs again, eating as I did and leaving a trail straight out of Hansel and Gretel. When I got to the bedroom, I put on my Keds and tied the laces. I was halfway down the stairs before I remembered the chamber pot. Even more awful than emptying it myself was the thought of Grandma or my mother doing it. So I returned to the bedroom, knelt down, and pulled it out. There wasn't much inside, but I carried it carefully anyway, holding it out from my chest like a chalice. When I reached the back bedroom, I put it on the bureau and opened the window, looking in every direction to make sure nobody was watching. Then I lifted the pot over the sill and dumped its contents into the bushes below.

That done, I raced back downstairs, past Grandma, and out the door. My destination was a shed next to an unused outhouse that stood next to the chicken coops. All these many years later, I can still smell those birds. I breathed through my mouth as I flipped open the latch and slipped into the shadows. When my eyes got used to the dark, I saw the weapons leaning against the plank wall: the plastic-and-tin Daisy Red Ryder BB gun that my father had taught me how to shoot on the prairie along the tracks and next to it the beautiful, wood-stocked, blued-barrel CO_2 pellet gun my parents had gotten me for my birthday. It could have passed for a .22, and over the first fifty yards or so it packed the wallop of a hunting rifle. It also had a clear advantage when it came to stealth, since the only report it made when it fired was a little puff of breath.

I seized the pellet rifle and trotted off, holding it at port arms the way my father had taught me. We used to go through the whole Manual of Arms together, both the regular Army way and the flashier National Guard style. My father snapped the weapon smartly through right-shoulder, left-shoulder, order, and present arms, ending at parade rest. It was the first time I really could imagine that he had been a soldier. For myself, I liked the National Guard way. This left my father disconsolate.

As I came out of the shed, Grampa was opposite me behind his mower.

"Going hunting?" he called.

"Nah," I said. "Just messing around."

Grampa looked at me as if he still had enough boy in him to know better.

They said you could find muskrats in the ditches along the cornfields north of town. They said you could find weasels. The bounty on these was higher than on crows, which were in any event too smart to let a boy sight in on them. You received payment by turning in the varmint's carcass at the general store. At least that was what my second cousin had told me, making it sound as full of glory as the National Guard. So I was determined to bag myself a fierce weasel because anybody had the guts to shoot a bird.

Behind the church lay an immensity of cornfields cut through by a ditch big enough to require a culvert under the C&EI tracks. I let myself down the bank until my Keds touched the moist matting of grass at the bottom. A few hops from rock to rock carried me across the slow-moving water.

I saw no sign of weasels in any direction, so I decided to lie in ambush, cradling my rifle across my lap, safety off for speed, finger on the trigger, waiting for the moment when a weasel was foolish enough to show itself. I sat perfectly still for what felt like hours, then the fidgets got the better of me. I brought my rifle up and fired at a stick twenty or thirty yards away. I thought I saw it jump and counted this as a kill. Then I lay back again and waited.

There were burrows everywhere that must have led to underground quarry. Did weasels live in burrows? I should have asked Grampa, who knew about everything. It had been Grampa who had taught me to recognize the long, curving berm in a lawn that meant a mole. Technically speaking, I guess I had already killed my first mammal when a spring-loaded trap I had set drove a sharp trident into the soil as the mole passed beneath. But this was no more satisfying than catching a mouse. I only knew I had succeeded by the mole guts on the tines.

Out in the sun nothing was moving except the water. There weren't even any fish in the ditch because between rains it often completely dried up. I stood and walked downstream in the direction of the railroad tracks. Maybe on the other side, where the ditch ran through a stand of trees, I could find varmints.

When I got to the tracks, I stopped on the ballast and found a good rock to place on the rail. It balanced neatly on the steel surface that had been polished by the trains. My mother always warned me not to place even so much as an old penny in the way of the big diesels that roared through Abbeville. "You don't want to be responsible for a wreck, do you?" she said. But I had done it anyway, dozens of times, once Grampa had sneaked me a peek at his collection of coins the trains had turned into foil.

Down the way, the preacher's wife emerged from the back door of her house, crossed the clearing, and took the stairs to the church basement. She did not look in my direction. I crossed the tracks and made my way to the grove of trees, sure I would only slay the prize by tracking it to its lair.

When the ditch entered the grove, it widened, making scummy pools behind fallen tree limbs. I found a small burrow, but it probably belonged to a snake. Beyond lay a thicket that could have served as something's den. But when I reached it, I found absolutely no sign of life.

Back home in Park Forest I often retreated to a little woods a block away from our house. Sometimes I would scare up a pheasant in the prairie beyond it or see a rabbit running away. It never seemed particularly wild there, but compared to this it teemed like the African savannah.

To get to the other side of the water, I had to walk across a fallen log, using my rifle like a tightrope walker's pole. I was more than halfway there when I started to get into trouble. My toe stubbed on a big knot. The rifle began to teeter wildly. The next thing I knew I was lying in the fetid water.

It wasn't deep, but it soaked my pants and one side of my shirt. Thankfully, the barrel of my rifle stayed dry, but the stock had sunk deep into the mud. I leaned on it to get upright and eventually was able to reach dry ground. But as I did, my foot pulled out of my shoe, leaving it mired in the sucking muck.

Some hunter! I looked down at my pants and could not help thinking of a little boy who has peed himself. Then suddenly I felt someone watching me. I turned. A squirrel had me fixed in its gaze. The first quarry of the day, and it was stalking me.

As I raised the muddy rifle butt to my shoulder, the squirrel lit out. I fired but came nowhere close to it. Before I had a chance to fire again, it had put a tree trunk between us and scampered up it.

Losing a squirrel was no reason to cry. Getting my pants wet was no reason. Not having a clean hand or shirt cuff to wipe the tears was the least reason of all.

Eventually I had the presence of mind to rinse the rifle butt free of mud and get moving again. When I reached the tracks, I heard the preacher's wife inside the church singing Elvis's "Love Me Tender." Up in the belfry I thought I saw the shape of a hawk. Sure, it was a bird, but a big one that would bring a bounty. I raised my rifle and began to plant my feet, but before I could get my sights on the predator I flinched. The rifle fired a puff of CO_2. Then came a shattering of glass. The woman's song turned into a scream.

When I lifted my burning foot, the bee I had stepped on was writhing. Fear overcame pain, and I limped into the cornfield as fast as my injury allowed.

As I fled down the rows, the leaves ripped at my arms. I kept going until I could not even tell which direction the sun was. It didn't matter. At least I was getting away from the scene of the crime.

The farther I went, the more the pain forced its way back through the fear. My foot felt as though it had swollen to five times its normal size. It was a surprise when I pulled off my sock and saw that the damage was pretty much localized in my big toe.

It hurt too much to put the sock back on. When I stood up, I found that I could walk painlessly, though awkwardly, by staying on my heel. The trouble was, I had no idea where to go. The corn loomed two feet over my head. Every direction, the rows looked exactly the same. I began walking, having no idea whether it was toward safety or more trouble.

Becoming lost was no reason to cry. Shooting the preacher's wife was no reason to cry. Nor even having to face my mother. I sat down in the middle of nowhere and bawled.

I only stopped when the ground began rumbling beneath me. The wail of the horn rose in pitch as the train took the turn toward Abbeville and picked up speed.

The sound showed me the way out of the maze. But when I got up I suddenly remembered the stone I had put on the track. I tried to move fast so I could kick the stone away before the train got there, but my stung foot hobbled me. I reached the edge of the field just as the diesel arrived, and I imagined the big engine's flat nose rising up and then crashing to earth, a hundred cars behind it flying off the tracks. I slid back a few feet into the corn. The engineer leaned on the horn as it passed over the stone without so much as a shiver.

As its hundred cars rattled past, I sneaked back to Grampa and Grandma's house. It appeared that nobody had been in the shed after me, so I was able to wipe the last of the mud off the stock of the rifle and replace it next to the BB gun. When I was finished, I retraced my path. I had to retrieve my lost shoe.

When I got to the ditch, I crouched so as to be hidden by the banks. When I reached the tracks, I heard the preacher's voice coming my way. I had no choice but to step into the slimy water and hide in the culvert.

At first it didn't scare me. Then I thought I felt something flitting across my ankles, and it was all I could do not to cry out.

When I had gotten about halfway through the tunnel, the preacher's voice boomed through it the way it did on Sundays, full of hell's fire.

"The wretch must have stood right about here," he said.

I froze.

"Look," he said. "Some fool kids were putting rocks on the tracks again. I bet it's the same ones that did the shooting."

"You see any other rocks?" said another voice I didn't recognize. "Because here comes the 11:02."

I felt a deep, muffled rumble beneath his words, growing in intensity. Up above, on the beautiful surface of the Earth, I could pretty much judge a train's distance by the sound. But down here in hell everything echoed and was magnified. When the preacher delivered his sermons, I had never really been able to imagine eternal punishment, but suddenly I knew that it would be just like what I was feeling in the culvert: ordinary things raised to the level of terror.

I hunkered down more, as if another inch of clearance would save me. The noise became excruciating. I put my hands over my ears, but it did not help. My whole body had become an eardrum.

Finally the engine passed and the noise abated. Now was my chance to get away, covered by the passing boxcars. I waded out of the culvert and moved toward the grove of trees as fast as my sore foot would let me. I quickly found my lost shoe and rinsed it as well as I could in the stagnant water. It squished as I limped my way back toward the house. The coldness actually made the sting feel a little better.

This time I went in plain view, hoping to be seen—wet and filthy, but unarmed. When I got near the house, Grampa was hauling fallen twigs to a big pile out back of the school for burning. I suddenly remembered that he had seen me taking the rifle in the morning. I was sunk. He gave me a big wave and that smile of his. Even from a distance I must have looked like one of the condemned.

When I reached the house, I took off my shoes and went directly to the bathroom, passing Grandma on the fly.

"Oh, Lordy, what did you get into?" she said.

I started filling the tub, then bolted upstairs to get fresh clothes. By the time I returned the bath was ready. Of course, there was no way to make the Keds clean again.

Soon my parents returned.

"Did you hear about all the excitement at the church?" my mother asked. She was looking directly at me.

"Excitement?" said Grandma.

"Somebody put a hole through one of the stained-glass windows," my mother said.

A wave of relief came over me. At least the hole hadn't been in the preacher's wife.

"Was it one of ours?" Grandma asked. At some point in the distant past they had somehow been able to pay for three. Sometimes I would look at the plaques under them, Grampa's name on one, Grandma's on another, and my mother's on the third.

"It was the Schlagels'," my mother said, "but you can be sure we'll be called upon to help pay for fixing it."

"It won't take much," Grampa said, winking at me in a way nobody else could see. "I took a look. A little lead work and it'll be as good as new."

"Do they know who did it?" Grandma asked.

"Anybody here have any ideas?" my mother said. I had to force myself not to look away from her.

"I fell into the ditch north of the Hagens' place," I said. "In the trees there. My shoes and clothes got dirty. I'm sorry." I put one true statement after another, which meant I didn't lie.

"The ditch runs behind the church," my mother said.

"Maybe you saw something," said Grandma.

"A squirrel," I said.

"Squirrels don't shoot out windows," my mother said. As I used true statements to deceive, she used them to annoy.

"Did you have your pellet rifle?" my father asked.

Before I had a chance to figure how to answer that one, Grampa stepped in.

"I saw him come back," he said. "I've seen rats along Otter Creek that looked cleaner. But he didn't have the rifle."

I didn't look at him for fear that the gratitude on my face would give us away. Today I wonder whether it was his willingness to stand up for a fool that had gotten him in all the trouble.

"It had to have scared poor Mrs. Rose half to death," my mother said.

"She scares kind of easy," said Grampa.

"What were you doing in the ditch anyway, George?" my mother asked.

"Looking for a little adventure," Grampa said. "Leave the boy be."

"Boys mean trouble," said my mother.

"George," Grampa said, "when you are a lad it's your lot to be under a constant cloud of suspicion."

"A good thing, too," said my mother.

"When I have a little boy, I'm going to trust him," I said, guilt and pride all tossed together.

"That would make me a grandfather," said my father.

"It's honest work," Grampa grinned.

10

THE WAR IN EUROPE TOUCHED ABBEVILLE early, first driving up the price the farmers got for their grain, then tearing the town apart. The French hated Woodrow Wilson and wanted the United States to intervene immediately to take back their homeland from what they called "the Hun." The Germans, many of whose kin had left the Old Country specifically to avoid conscription, wanted neutrality at all costs.

Karl tried to stay out of the debate altogether, but he could not avoid its effects. Before the war he had begun to win French farmers from the south end over to his elevator. Now the momentum reversed. Despite the financial advantages Karl offered, the French were beginning to return to their own.

Meantime, Karl's situation at home had darkened. Cristina was not barren, but something was terribly wrong. The year before, she had become pregnant. It was a difficult delivery, desperately premature, and though Cristina had summoned the strength to survive it, Karl Jr. was so tiny that he did not have a chance. They buried him in the graveyard Karl had fenced as a young man.

"It will be all right," he told Cristina.

"I think it is because I want it too much," she wept.

"We both do," he said.

As they kept trying without success, Karl began to feel that somehow he owed a debt to fortune, that Cristina's grief was the price of his success.

One spring morning they were having breakfast on the porch, a breeze blowing in the fresh smells of newly plowed soil sprouting with life. Then another smell came. Cristina stood and pointed to smoke rising behind the elevator.

"Oh, my God!" she said.

Karl ran down the steps and raced across the prairie. A small crowd had gathered on Main Street, where an oily fire smoldered in front of the bank. Old Henry Mueller stood there, along with Will Hoenig, Georges Chartiens, Pierre Cordeaux, and Robert Schlagel. As Karl drew closer, he saw that their attention was not on the fire but on something beyond it.

The crowd parted as he crossed the street. That was when he saw it. In a different context the straw figure might not have frightened a crow. The effigy was dressed in a suit, vest, shirtfront, and tie. A sign pinned on the shirt said simply, "La Boche."

The thing swung by the neck from a cord strung over the electrical light above the door of the bank. Its head, a simple bag packed with straw and painted with a crude, cruel face, hung limply to one side. Karl walked up and yanked it down. The head pulled off and rolled to Chartiens's feet.

"Do you know who did this, Georges?" Karl asked.

"It does not matter," said Chartiens. "It is a blot on all of us."

Karl threw the figure into the smoldering fire. The straw burst into flame.

"Go home, everyone," Karl said. "Let this burn out."

"I'm not sure it will," said Mueller.

For weeks afterward the mark of that day lay before his eyes every time he entered or left the bank—a dark scorch upon the earth. Eventually he dug it up and turned it under, leaving a mound of fresh dirt. Within days an idea began to form.

When he wrote for information, he gave the bank as a return address so Cristina would not be alarmed. One response came from Donellan and Shaw Ambulance Service. A few days later the *Trib* carried a story datelined Paris about the valiant American lads of the organization, who were putting it on the line on behalf of the British, French, and Italian doughboys in the trenches. Karl took it as a sign.

He told Cristina that night.

"You've given up on me," she cried.

"It will be one year," he said. "No more. I promise."

"I am already past the time," she said.

"Maybe what I'm doing will lift the curse," he said.

"There is no curse, Karl," she said. "The curse is me. You will go to France and find someone else."

"There will never be anyone but you," Karl said. "You know that isn't why I need to go."

"To help save the French?" Cristina said. "They're the ones who hung that awful thing in front of the bank."

"It was one or two men."

"But they all know who it was," she said.

"It isn't so easy to see into other people's hearts," Karl said.

Cristina spoke her next words so softly that Karl could barely hear them.

"I can't see into yours anymore," she said.

Opinion in town was divided when Karl let people know of his plan. Simon Prideaux said it was a sly trick to get customers, and it was a fact that a number of the French who had left Karl did come back. The Germans were puzzled.

"You are almost forty, Karl, too old for such folly," said old Henry Mueller. "And anyway, it's not our war."

"It will be," Karl said.

"I'd worry about leaving a pretty wife all alone," said Mueller.

"We'll be fine," said Karl.

"And if you get killed?" Mueller said.

"I won't," said Karl.

"But why take the risk?" Mueller asked.

Karl did not even try to explain the intensely physical relationship he felt between the risk and what he hoped would be its reward.

As the time of his departure approached, he and Cristina somehow rediscovered the closeness and joy that they had lost to trying. It made leaving more difficult, but it was sweeter than anything they had felt since the death of their son.

KARL DID NOT LEARN WHAT CAME OF IT
for many months because Cristina was too
superstitious to write him about it. Only when the baby was nearly
due did she send him a letter with the wonderful news. In the meantime, Karl had sailed across the Atlantic, passed through Paris, and
ended up mired in Verdun.

When he finally got her letter, his first impulse was to return home
immediately, but then he became seized with doubt. If he short-
changed fortune now, what had happened to Karl Jr. could happen
again. So he stayed, tending not so much to the living as to the dead.

Many days he had to drive the stiff, bloating, soul-fled remains of
French soldiers wrapped in canvas to their last resting place, a field
well behind the lines, to be laid in a neat grid of graves. But then it
rained torrentially and there was no way to dig a hole deep enough to
keep the corpses from floating to the surface. Still, you could not leave
the dead where they fell for the artillery shells to bury and dig up
again, bury and dig up.

"What do you expect me to do with those?" said the French Army corporal at the gate of the cemetery, water cascading off his helmet.

"What is right," said Karl.

His French came easily now that he used it all the time. Flawless would not be the word, *sans défaut*. The academicians in Paris would have scowled at his soldier argot, but it was good enough for him to pass as Charles Pietre.

Of course, at first there was no mistaking him as anything but a Yank. The Frenchmen he had come to help had made fun of him, but they never suspected his origins were with the Hun.

"Do what is right, eh?" said the French corporal. "Nothing is right in this place."

The horses shivered and took a couple of steps backward. Karl pulled up on the reins.

"What do you propose I do with them?" said Karl, gesturing over his shoulder to the cargo in the wagon with its big red cross.

The corporal looked at him with the expression used by every banker who has ever refused a needy man a loan. Karl climbed down off the wagon. The corporal moved faster than you might have thought the mud would permit and put out his hand to keep Karl from opening the rear door.

"Do you expect me to take them back to the trenches?" said Karl.

He pulled sharply on the door of the wagon, surprising the corporal, whose hand slipped on the wet surface. When the door swung open, the smell struck like a blow. As Karl reached in to grab one of the corpses by the boot, he heard the unmistakable tick of metal against metal.

"Are you ready to die for them?" the corporal said.

When Karl moved away from the door, it swung shut of its own weight. He climbed into the box and picked up the reins.

"Tell the others," said the corporal.

"Maybe I will tell them to come armed," said Karl.

He twitched the reins and got the horses started. They were not eager to move, but he maneuvered them in a wide circle past the corporal, who kept his pistol trained on Karl.

The rain pinged off Karl's helmet like shrapnel and rolled frigid down his back. The horses pulled the wagon with as little sense of where they were headed as their driver. Then, through the gray curtain of rain and war smoke, he made out the shadow of a spire. He gave the reins a snap. The horses' gait picked up for a moment, then settled back.

When he reached the church, Karl alighted and secured the horses to the trunk of a dead tree. He did what he could on the wet steps to clean the mess off the bottom of his boots, then pulled open the heavy wooden door of the sanctuary and stepped inside. The only light came from the votive candles.

"Hello!" Karl called. His voice echoed. Beyond it he could hear the rain pounding against the roof high above, the rumble of distant guns. "Is anybody here?"

Something moved in the shadows.

"Hello there," he called again in French.

"Calm yourself," came a tiny, ancient voice in reply. "God can hear a pin drop. There is no use bellowing."

Now he could see a small figure coming toward him.

"The guns must deafen Him," Karl said.

The man dragged his left foot. When he laughed, it came to Karl from several directions at once, like birds in the rafters.

"My little trick," the man said. "I am sure the masons arranged the effect to suggest His omnipresence. And, of course, to frighten and delight the children."

When the man stepped closer to the light, Karl could see that he was wearing a long black soutane. The gold cross hanging at his heart was large. It caught the glow of the candles and sparkled.

"You have come a long way," said the *curé*.

"The battlefield is not so far," said Karl.

"You have an accent from nowhere," the *curé* said. "I have heard certain Canadians, but it is not even that exactly. You have come such a distance that I have never heard anyone quite like you before."

"America," said Karl, and the word was sweet on his lips.

"Ah," said the *curé*. "Tell me, what were you fleeing?"

His thin lips bore the slightest semblance of a smile.

"Fortune," Karl said. "I have had great success in everything but starting a family. My son died only a week after he was born. I thought maybe it was because I'd had been rewarded too much and risked too little. Now I have received a letter from my wife that she is pregnant. I suppose that by this time the birth has happened. I have no way of knowing."

"Then why are you here?" the *curé* asked.

"I am afraid that anything I do might curse us again," he said. He was beginning to sweat in his greatcoat. "Do you mind if I take this off?"

"So long as you also take that metal thing off your head," said the *curé*.

Karl reached up and snatched off the helmet, which had become such a part of him that he had forgotten he had it on.

"I have the remains of several soldiers in my wagon," he said. "I need to give them a proper burial."

"There are military cemeteries," said the *curé*.

"I was turned away," said Karl. "The man at the gate said the weather was too inclement."

"How ungenerous it was of these soldiers," said the *curé*, "to give their lives for France on one of its least attractive days."

"I cannot bring them back to the front," said Karl.

"Of course not," said the *curé*, "but they can find rest anywhere, you know. The soul flies up. What is left is the chrysalis of the moth."

At first Karl had trouble with the word in French.

"The what?" he asked. "Excuse me. My American vocabulary."

"You know a moth?" said the *curé*, patiently, joining his hands backward at the thumbs to make a pair of wings.

"Like an angel?" said Karl.

"It lives at night and is attracted to the flame," said the *curé*.

"Ah, yes," said Karl. "Now I understand. The soul flies upward toward the flame."

"Here, come with me."

To the right, through a big open wooden door carved with figures, stretched a dark corridor. At the far end light spilled out from a doorway. Half-a-dozen candles flickered in a tiny room. In the corner of it glowed the embers of a cooking fire. Karl felt his collar beginning to dry in the warmth, the feeling coming back into his toes. Above the stove hung an iron cauldron on a pivot. The *curé* limped to it and looked into its depths, as if he might see the future there. Then he went to a large earthen jar that sat on the floor, covered with a circular wooden cover. From it he ladled a fair quantity of water into the cauldron, which he then lifted off its pivoting arm and placed directly on top of the stove. From a pile of logs he chose two and set them atop the embers, which he blew to life. The sparks flew up.

"The warmth," Karl said. "You are very kind."

"It is not often that I have a visit from an American who has been entrusted with France's glorious dead," said the *curé*.

Karl was surprised at the sarcasm.

"You do not see glory in their sacrifice?" he asked.

The *curé* ladled some steaming water into a cup, into which he then spilled a quantity of tea leaves. When he had stirred them under, he handed Karl the cup.

"Theirs is only sacrifice," he said. "The glory belongs, as all glory does, to France."

"Had she any choice but to defend herself?" said Karl.

The *curé* repeated the process with a second cup, sipping it before he answered.

"Did you have a choice in coming here?" he asked.

"I could have just left the bodies somewhere," Karl said. His eyes slipped to the floor. "I actually thought about it."

"I mean coming to France," said the *curé*.

"I felt a powerful need," Karl said.

"And now?" said the *curé*.

"I'm not sure anymore what good I do," Karl said. "They die with or without me."

"You were drawn to the suffering," said the *curé*. "You flew toward the flame and have been touched by it. We will put your friends in the catacombs. Perhaps we will find something on their persons that will tell us whom to notify so that their kin will know where they have found peace. Now, finish your tea and we will begin."

The *curé* insisted on following him to the wagon, despite the difficulty he had walking. Karl threw the first corpse onto his shoulder.

"The least we can do is to show the way with the cross," the *curé* said, carrying it high on the end of a staff.

Methodically, they moved all six bodies to the antechamber of the catacombs. The *curé* lit torches that angled upward from its stone walls.

"Well, now," he said. "Let us see the Germans' work."

He took a small knife and slit the crude stitching that held together the winding sheets. A wave of stench hit them as the canvas fell away. The *curé* did not recoil. It was as if he breathed different air.

He pulled open the cloth slowly, revealing a sight to which Karl had become all too accustomed. Half the man's head was a pulp.

"French pride and German surgery," said the *curé*.

He pulled the cloth open farther until he could slide his hand in to reach the pockets of the dead soldier's tunic. From one he withdrew a letter, which he opened and moved closer to one of the torches.

"It is from this man's wife," he said.

He returned to the body and put the canvas back in place. Then he took one of the torches down and led the way into the catacombs.

"These were here long before the church," he said as the light of the flame flickered across cobwebbed piles of bones, occasionally illuminating a skull. "We do not know who all of these people were. We presume they were Christians, though the worms feast on such distinctions."

Karl carried the soldier's dead weight across his arms. At times he had to move sideways. The corridors came together at such odd and unpredictable angles that soon he was lost.

"Here," the *curé* said. "This shall be our chamber of the Great War. It shall memorialize the coming of a new century. I am pretty sure this husband and the others will not be the last soldiers to be buried here."

Karl laid the body on an open shelf, then slid it in as far as he could.

"Yes," said the *curé*. "We must conserve space, for France is very, very proud."

They repeated the process six times. Karl suggested after the second that they bring the rest and do the rite for all of them together. The *curé* would not hear of it.

"Let each become an individual again," he said, "as he was seen by his loved ones and as he is now being seen by God."

When the last man had found his bed of stone, they returned with the fire and the cross to the room with the woodstove.

"I must leave, Father," he said, then paused. "But first I would like you to hear my confession."

"How long has it been?" said the *curé*.

"I am a Protestant," Karl said. "I do not even know the proper way."

"Come with me."

In one corner of the nave stood several wooden cabinets.

"I will enter first," said the *curé*. "This will preserve your anonymity."

He disappeared. Karl paused, then opened the second door. It was as dark inside as it had been in the catacombs. For some reason he suddenly felt very cold.

Something moved, wood sliding against wood.

"You may begin now," the *curé* said softly. "Do not worry about form, my son. Only think of cleansing your soul."

"I am German, Father," Karl said in his best French.

KARL FOLLOWED THE RIVER back through town and past the useless cemetery. The rain had abated. The guns on the far side of the ridgeline spoke intermittently.

Instead of turning right where the road forked back to the front, Karl kept close to the river on a much less rutted path that led into a stand of trees. Some of the branches hung low enough to scrape the top of the wagon, making a hollow sound.

The river ran thunderously high. Karl moved the wagon close to the spate, which was so loud it even covered the sound of the guns. For a moment he could imagine No-Man's-Land washed clean, renewing itself, life coming back. Maybe that was genius of the story of Christ, uniting mortal humanity with nature's recurrence. Winters end. Wars end. Prosperity follows panic, rise after fall.

"You are guilty of nothing, son," the *curé* had said through the confessional screen. "We were all born something. French. German. American. Not one of us had any say. Go home. Be with your lovely wife and your new child. And as to your fear, remember that God's grace is nothing you need to repay, nor is punishment the proof of sin.

This is the first great mystery, my son, and it is only made bearable by the second, which is love.

"You see," the cure said, "fortune is not the outcome of a test. Good or bad, it is the test."

WHEN KARL REACHED the ambulance corps headquarters, the colonel was waiting for him.

"Did you stop at a bordello?" he asked.

Karl recounted the lengths he had gone to in order to give the French soldiers a proper burial, the refusal of the corporal at the cemetery, the decency of the *curé*.

"Are you sure the men were all Roman Catholics?" asked the colonel. Always a question. Just like his father. Karl could have pulled one hundred men back alive from No-Man's-Land under fire and the colonel would have asked him whether he had remembered to stow the stretchers properly.

"The *curé* will contact the next of kin," Karl said. "It will be taken care of, no thanks to the Army of France."

"Very unorthodox," said the colonel.

He was as fastidious as a man could be in a world of mud. A thick brown belt cinched his olive jacket at the shoulder and waist. From his lapel hung a chain and on the end of it a pince-nez.

"I am resigning from the corps," Karl said.

"Well," said the colonel, "I'm afraid you will have to be a coward later. At the moment your services are immediately required."

Karl made his way through the narrow maze of communications trenches toward the point in the front line where a scouting party had gone over the top and not returned. He found two others from the ambulance corps, and together they located one more.

"We'd better get started," said Karl.

The clouds were breaking in the west, the afternoon sun turning them into great, billowing fires. At some point, this splendid show would make a perfect silhouette of anyone crossing the parapet, but for now the sun was too high for that.

"You are Pietre," said the oldest of his companions.

"I used to be," Karl said.

The older man accepted that. No one who came to this place remained who he had been.

The other two were younger. One, he recalled being told, had been a fugitive in the United States.

"I have forgotten your name," Karl said.

"It's just as well," said the fugitive. "A name is just something you drag along behind you in the mud."

Karl paired up with him. One person could pull a stretcher forward, but two was the rule for carrying a man back.

"Here we go," said Karl.

They heaved up a stretcher and see-sawed it on the parapet. Then they pulled themselves over the top.

No gunfire met them. This might have meant they had lucked into a position with a little bit of cover. Or it might only have meant that the German riflemen at the strongpoint across No-Man's-Land had been dreaming of the *fräuleins* and had missed the shot. Karl crawled madly until he got to the bottom of a crater deep enough that he could not be seen from the German lines.

He would have been willing to stay there for a while, but the fugitive quickly made his way up and over the far wall. When Karl caught up with him in the next crater, the fugitive had positioned himself on the slope closest to the German guns. He had removed his helmet and was leaning his head sharply to the side to try to sneak a look over the lip of the hole with a single eye.

"Do you see him?" Karl whispered.

The sound of his voice touched off a loud wail from somewhere near them.

"Quiet, man!" Karl barked. "Pretend you are already dead so the *Boche* will lose interest in you."

Soon the cries softened to a moan. Eventually even the moaning stopped.

"Do you think he is dead?" Karl whispered.

"I think you told him to act as if he was," said the fugitive. "We can't very well leave him to die because he did what he was told."

"Most who have died," said Karl, "died for that reason."

The fugitive pulled himself a little higher up the crater wall and looked over the edge again.

"You go to that side. I'll go to this," he said. "Whoever reaches our man first will drag him back here to the stretcher."

Just as Karl and the fugitive rose, a big gun fired. The sound of it communicated through the earth. Then the whistle of the shell filled the sky. The explosion was off to their left. The next shell came before they had recovered from the shock wave. It hit on the right, and both of them knew what that meant. The gunner had them bracketed, and the next one would come in right on top of them. They scrambled madly up the bank. Karl had just made it out when he looked back and saw the fugitive lose his footing. The gun fired. There was no whistle. The world erupted in light. Then everything went black.

The first thing he saw when he came to was the dying sun. He did not know whether he had been unconscious for a few minutes or a few days. His head ached, but when he managed to get his arm out from under him and ran his hand over his face and through his hair, there was no blood. He did not move until the sun went behind the hills and the shadows crawled over him.

At the bottom of the crater lay the twisted, decapitated body of the fugitive. Karl put the remains on the stretcher. The enemy trenches were perhaps seventy-five yards away, dark and silent. He could barely make out the contour of the land, but he dug in with his elbow and heel to move himself and his burden in the other direction. Four yards. Five yards. He felt the earth sloping slightly upward, making his progress more difficult. His breath became labored, but soon he felt the verge of a hole. With one thrust, he was in it.

When he recovered his breath, he realized that this crater was too shallow to permit him to stand. He squinted into the shadows, felt the ground with his fingers. Mud and roots. Pieces of spent shrapnel. A rat, which skittered away. Karl soon found what it had been eating. The cloth under his fingers was heavy, the kind they used for greatcoats. He pulled his hand away.

He tried to visualize the path to the friendly trench line, then to the rear, then to the troop train, then finally to Cristina's warm, enveloping arms that would never let him go again. There would be more children. If it was God's will, they would populate Abbeville and consecrate it against all the evils of the world.

"Halt!" The word in German stopped Karl. He heard the voice of his father. "You! Frenchman! Put down your rifle and come here or I will kill you!"

The shadow of a helmet rose at the perimeter of the crater. Though he could not see it, Karl knew there would also be the muzzle of a rifle. His whole body shook and his voice cracked as he spoke the perfect truth.

"I am German," he said in his father's tongue.

12

THE TRAIN THEY PUT KARL IN PULLED nothing but boxcars used for hauling horses and men. He made his way stiffly to a far corner and lay down. Every time he moved, he disturbed the soldiers around him. As the train began to roll, a draft sent a chill through him like a fever, but it was not enough to blow away the smell of men who had just emerged from the mud.

Morning came. The sun cut through the slats. He saw two church spires rising into the perfect blue sky. One was closer than the other. At first they appeared stationary: two graceful fingers pointed toward heaven. But as the train continued to move, they began to converge, like the sights on a rifle. Beneath him the rails beat a steady tick-tick, tick-tick.

"YOU!" THE VOICE from the lip of the crater had shouted. "Come forward! Now!"

Then came the sound of a rifle bolt: tick-tick.

Karl did not move.

"I surrender," he whispered in German.

A rifle barked. In the flash he saw the eyes of the German soldier. Then he heard the sound of the man's helmet tumbling down the slope and splashing at the bottom of the pit.

A voice in French said, "Can you move?"

"Everyone is dead," Karl said.

"Stay where you are," said the voice. "We will come back for you."

Karl dreaded being alone again in the darkness. Machine-gun fire stuttered far off to the right. Then a long, eerie silence into which crept some kind of muffled rhythm from the direction of the dead German. Karl tried to disregard it. A flare went up, hissing. When it fell back to earth, the mud snuffed it out. Then in the silence the sound came back.

It could not have been the German's heart still beating. To hear Cristina's heart, Karl had to put his head directly onto her chest. In the light of the flare the German's body lay splayed out, rifle in hand, as inert as the earth. And yet the sound still came. Tick-tick. Tick-tick. Karl rubbed his ears. They distorted everything now, even his own breathing, which caught in his chest. Tick-tick.

When he reached the German, another flare swung above him, lighting the man's contorted face. Karl reached out his hand and touched the man's chest. Tick-tick. He pushed his hand inside the coat, where his fingers encountered metal.

As another flare came up, he extracted his hand. The eerie light glowed off the polished gold of a watchcase engraved with a pattern of hills and sun rays and sheaves of wheat. With his fingernail he flicked it open. The second hand steadily moved ahead.

"Time to go," said a voice in French. "Don't worry about your friend. Someone will drag him back."

Karl crawled up out of the hole and followed the Frenchman.

Whenever flares came, the two of them halted, face down, trying to merge with the mud. Eventually they were able to roll over the parapet of the forward trench line.

Karl did not pause even to clean himself. He immediately made his way through the communicating trenches to the Ambulance Corps headquarters, where he wrote out his resignation papers. From there he hitched a ride by lorry to the train station in Verdun. Fortune provided a troop train that was just boarding. The officers did not stand on ceremony when he proved with his papers and his English that he was not a deserter.

IN THE DISTANCE a farmhouse slowly fell behind the train until it was out of sight. In its place a pair of plain American steeples slid into view. The cross of the closer church appeared to reach higher into the perfect autumn sky. Karl leaned back in the plush seat and thought of the *curé,* the damp chill in the crypt, the fugitive, all the dead. They inhabited a different world than this vast Central Illinois landscape, which was protected from history by an ocean and hundreds of miles of farmland and forests. He watched the towers glide along beside the train, directing eye and heart to God.

He put his hand into his pocket and took out the watch, running his finger over the gold pattern, then snapping it open with his thumbnail. The inscription inside was in the kind of old-fashioned German cursive that generations of Schumpeters had used on the frontispieces of family Bibles. It simply said, "For Johann on his birthday, April 20, 1915." The dead German had been hardly more than a boy. Had his father given him the watch? Had it been from his new wife?

The watch said 4:35. Unless the C&EI timetable had changed, this meant that they were only twenty-four minutes from Abbeville, and some of that was for a stop in Kankakee. It had been a long time since he could say exactly when something was going to happen. He slipped the gold disk back into his vest pocket.

In its day perhaps the timepiece had predicted trains in Germany. Or perhaps Johann had grown up on the coast and used it to figure the tides. Maybe he was a baker, timing his loaves, or a brewer minding the yeast. Or even a farmer, bound by sunrise and sunset, the steady tilt and spin of the earth. Tick-tick. The rails clicked beneath Karl, the watch in his pocket, guiding him out of the past.

He had telegraphed from Uncle John's office the time he would arrive in Abbeville, and in response he had learned that he was the father of a baby girl. As the click of the rails slowed, his heart raced. From the shelf above the seat he pulled down the single, half-empty canvas bag with gifts from Paris. In the swaying vestibule he peered through a small window in the door. The intervals between fence posts lengthened. The church came into view, then his house. It was incredible that nothing had changed.

Then came Cristina's face and the baby, just as he had dreamt. Behind them it looked as though the whole town had come out, German and French alike. Some of the children held tiny American flags.

The crowd cheered as the porter appeared in the door and set down the step. Karl hesitated. Then he heard Cristina's voice.

"Karl!" she called.

Before he could get his footing, her arm was around him, the baby's head touching his face. He dropped his bag and held her, right there in front of everyone, and sobbed. The crowd applauded.

"You'll never go away again, will you?" Cristina said. "You must promise me that."

"I do," he said, just as he had the day they had wed.

13

T HE FIRST THING THEY DID WAS TO GIVE the child a name. Baby Schumpeter became Elizabeth. Within an hour they were calling her Betty. Karl loved to play with her, making funny faces, appearing and disappearing behind the edge of her crib. He loved just watching her, and she had an insatiable appetite for his affection, which grew in him the more he gave her.

In the businesses, he quickly fell back into his old routines, opening the bank in the morning, spending time at the elevator monitoring the telegraph when the trading day in the pits began, conferring with his brother, who liked to rise late after spending long nights with the politicians and officials who could influence where road construction contracts went.

"Be careful," Karl warned him. "Some of those fellas don't seem straight."

"Watch your own self," Fritz said. "I'm not the one who's got the county prosecutor's grudge."

Harley Ansel had done well for himself in private practice before turning to prosecuting criminals, but Karl never saw him, since Ansel now spent all his time in Potawatomi.

"That was a long time ago," Karl said.

Simon Prideaux sued for peace within a year. Things came together nicely. The deal Karl offered was that he and Fritz would take the French elevator in return for some cash plus a number of parcels of Schumpeter farmland. Prideaux haggled a bit over the cash, then accepted and thus became the first Frenchman to own property north of town. Soon one of his pretty daughters married one of the Hoenig boys and the whole family promptly began appearing in the evangelical church as if they had been born again.

Not long afterward America joined the war. French and Germans volunteered. Soon the hatred that had hung the effigy seemed cleansed in common sacrifice.

Then came the Spanish flu epidemic that put everyone in fear of anyone they didn't know and half of those they did. Because of his experience as sheriff, Karl was delegated to scare off the gypsy bands that showed up from time to time. Old Henry Mueller gave him a double-barreled shotgun to help him make the point. Karl accepted it but always left it at home. Instead he went to meet the caravans with food Cristina had canned and a little money from his own pocket. The gypsies gave Abbeville a wide berth, and folks credited Karl with keeping the epidemic at bay.

Meanwhile, a couple of decent crops and rising prices put money in everyone's pockets. The bank's deposits swelled, and so did its portfolio of loans. One of its bigger debtors was Fritz.

"I wouldn't lend him an umbrella on a rainy day," said Rose Stroeger, Karl's assistant at the bank. "He just uses the money to lord it over you. Fancy cars. Big vacations. And Edna's clothes. She tries her worst to make Cristina look plain."

"I am blessed with the love of a practical woman," Karl said.

Fritz was more than willing to let Karl manage the partnership businesses while he devoted his time to building roads that could handle the heavy implements the Schumpeter Bros. were selling.

"I hope he remembers to leave a little unpaved for tillage," Karl said.

When the war ended, prosperity did not. Karl ventured up to Chicago from time to time to consult with Uncle John, who assured him that the Republicans would drive the economy to heights no one had ever imagined.

"Imagination," he said. "That's what a man needs today. We are seeing a great transformation, driven by the gasoline engine and industrial ingenuity. The risk today is not losing your capital but being left behind."

On one of his trips Karl managed to locate Luella, who he was happy to learn had done all right for herself, landing both a decent job in a real estate firm and a fellow.

"We aren't married," Luella said.

"Yet," said Karl.

"As good as," Luella teased, her red hair lighting her eyes. On one of Karl's visits he met the man. Joe O'Toole was his name: big and brawny and obviously able to handle himself.

She never wanted to talk to Karl about the past, even when they were alone. Instead they would discuss the day's events, about which Luella always had a very un-Republican set of views.

As the years passed, Karl's parents' health began to fade. There was no question who would take care of them. Edna wasn't up to it, Fritz said. Cristina made a place for Karl's folks in the bedrooms where she and Karl had always slept. Her own father was slowing down, too, and Karl expected that he and Cristina would be living upstairs with Betty for quite a while.

But then Karl's father died, and in short order Cristina's father and both of their mothers succumbed. All this death seemed to cut off the top of Cristina's emotions. It was not that they did not find happiness together anymore. It was just that they did not know joy.

"The way to end her grieving," Fritz told him, "is to take her to Paris. Edna and I are going in the spring."

"Beautiful city," Karl said. "But it's a little dear."

Instead he began to plan a trip to the river where he had grown into manhood. He ordered maps that showed the roads as tiny capillaries reaching into the great, empty expanses of the north. He ordered from Sears, Roebuck the things they would need—fishing gear, camping equipment, oilcloth bags to keep their things dry in the canoe, clothing that would hold up against rain and thorn.

"The feel of a cold running river," he said.

"I can get that by putting my hand under the pump," Cristina said.

He turned to Betty.

"There are eagles," he said. "American eagles like on the top of the flagpole. There are beavers and badgers. There are bears."

"Bears?" Betty said, lighting up.

"Not to hug," Cristina said. "These are real, with teeth and claws."

"They wouldn't hurt you, would they?" she said.

"Hurt Goldilocks?" said Karl. "I wouldn't let them."

By the time the weather warmed up, Karl had put his business affairs in order. Rose had a power of attorney giving her authority to act in his stead on any bank or partnership matter.

"For Fritz's sake it would be best if you used it sparingly," Karl said. "You remember how he resented my turning to you when I went off to the war."

"For your sake it would be best if Fritz stayed in Paris," she said.

The car trip north took the better part of a week. As they grew closer to their destination, the plains gave way to rolling hills.

"Are these the mountains?" Betty asked.

"I had no idea there were places like this," said Cristina.

"Imagine it filled with towering trees," said Karl.

"It's a pity you cut them all down," said Cristina.

"Money can be like fire," said Karl.

The road to the place Karl had rented was, at its best, little more than a path beaten into the grass. The closer they got, the bumpier it became.

"My God," said Karl. "This is where I paid the Indians."

He pulled up next to a clapboard cabin. Betty raced in and claimed a room upstairs. Cristina chose the bedroom on the ground floor. To Karl's delight, in it stood only one big cast-iron bed.

When he had brought everything inside, Karl felt his way down a crude set of rock steps to where the river stretched out a full seventy-five yards downstream. Along the eroded banks the trees were thin and whippy. In other places grass had moved into the sunlight where the white pine had fallen. Down the way a high bank had been sliding little by little into the water, spreading a choking blanket of sand over the lovely gravel beds where fish used to spawn.

"Is it what you had hoped?" asked Cristina.

She looked down at a wooden rack where two canoes lay bottom up. A wasp flew out from beneath one of them.

"I pray you don't expect me to handle one of those things on the river," she said.

"After dark I'd better move that nest so Betty doesn't get herself stung," he said.

As they stood there, the river whispered.

"I don't know what it is, but it draws me," Karl said.

Later he strung one of the new fly rods made of split cane. Handing it to Betty, he directed her down to the riverbank, then situated her so she would have a clean backcast and not need to worry about getting snagged in a bush. He showed her the way you used the weight of the line to flex the rod tip to throw the fly. At first her cast died in a mess in the water in front of her, but very quickly she began to get the knack.

"She's a natural," he told Cristina afterward as he peeled potatoes for dinner.

The meal was hearty, more farm than forest. They ate on the porch, the lantern drawing in scores of moths to the screens the way the boom was drawing in people. Betty got up to examine one, then went outside to look at it from the other side.

When she returned to where they were sitting, she held out her right index finger. On it was a tiny white patch.

"Let's see," said Karl.

"It's like a doily sewn by elves," she said.

Just then he saw a shadow darting nearby. His hand shot out. When he brought it back in front of him and opened it, a large brown insect with a long, curving body slowly stretched its gauzy wings.

"You seem to have let in a mayfly," he said.

"It doesn't look like a fly," said Betty.

"That's because you're thinking of houseflies," said Karl. "For a year this creature grew from its mother's egg into a nymph deep in the river. A few hours ago it shed its casing and swam to the surface. It waved its wings in the current until they were dry, then leaped from the water into the air for the first time. In a couple of days it will mate. The females will lay their eggs on the water and fall dead."

"How sad," said Betty.

"A mayfly has only one purpose, which is to change itself from one form to another in order to propagate its kind," said Karl. "It is not like a person, who needs to change the world."

Karl handled the cleanup as Cristina went upstairs to settle Betty into bed. When he finished he went outside again, walking as far as the bend in the river, then a little beyond until he could not see the light of the cabin anymore. Above him in the total darkness millions of stars spread across the sky. Down below, the river hush was broken from time to time by the sound of a rising fish.

At a gas station where they had stopped on the way in, Karl had asked the portly mechanic with a thick Dutch accent how the fishing was these days. All the grayling had been destroyed in the logging, the mechanic said. Brookies weren't that easy to find anymore, either. Fat German brown trout had taken over. "Germans," he said.

The next morning Karl slid a canoe into the water, held it steady for Cristina and Betty, and then began to paddle. Everywhere new trees shaded the banks, mostly spruce and deciduous varieties. Here grew a stand of conifers, one of them leaning off the bank so that its bottom branches swept the current. There stood some lovely fresh birches, grown safely above the reach of the deer. Where the trees hadn't filled back in, high grass had grown so lush that Cristina said it was hard to believe that this place had ever suffered the slash of steel.

"Will we see varmints, Daddy?" asked Betty.

"None we can't handle," said Karl.

Up ahead, the banks closed in and the riverbed went into a steeper drop. The water became choppy.

"Hold on," Karl warned.

They took the bumps easily. Betty whooped. Karl saw Cristina's knuckles go white on the gunwales. He paddled harder, biting into the rushing water to keep them in the center of the chute. In less than a minute the water flattened out again.

"I hope that's the last of that," Cristina said.

"I hope not," said Betty.

The second set of rapids came a mile or so downstream. This one rumbled past a high clay bank.

"Karl!" Cristina shouted when they were on the verge.

"Here goes!" he shouted back.

The canoe bounced. Karl kept paddling. Cristina was holding the gunwale with one hand and Betty's life jacket with the other. Karl remembered doing this stretch of the river many times, once on three strapped-together logs. Of all the places he had seen so far, this one was the least changed.

"That wasn't so bad, was it?" he said.

The water quickly flattened out into a great, moving sheet of amber.

"Look," Karl said, pointing. A fish rose, leaving an expanding ring.

"He was a big one," Karl said.

"Can we catch him?" said Betty, fairly bouncing in her place.

"There will be plenty of others," Karl said.

His plan was to get as far as the riffles upriver of the rollway before stopping. The casting would be easy there, where he remembered the river flowing through a wide meadow so there would be no trees or bushes to tangle them up. It was near the place where he had lost a fish and the Indian had speared one. This time he would, by God, get his fish to the net.

Before that, however, he had to maneuver the canoe through the most treacherous water they were going to face. Up ahead the whole riverbed tilted to the left, dumping most of the flow through a narrow, rushing chute on the outside of the bend. At the far end lay an obstacle course of fallen limbs and low, overhanging branches.

As they approached, he pulled his paddle into the boat, letting the flat, silent current carry them. Then he reached down and freed the other paddle from under Betty's foot.

"Here," he said, holding it out to Cristina handle first. "Make short, scooping strokes, all on the left side of the canoe. That will help pull us toward the inside shore and away from the snag."

As he demonstrated, the canoe swung into the shallow water. Gravel scraped the bottom.

"What if I drop the paddle?" Cristina asked.

"It will float downriver and eventually get hung up in a snag," he said. "We'll be able to retrieve it."

"What will happen to us without the paddle?" she said.

"Just don't try to stand up," he said. "No matter what."

He could feel the current pulling them into its crease. White water was visible ahead. If the river had been slightly higher, it might have been possible to stay way over to the right, but the water there was so shallow that the gravel would have torn up the bottom of the canoe.

"Here we go," Karl said.

They were pulled steadily to the left even with both adults paddling at full strength against the drift. The canoe wobbled as Betty shifted her weight up front.

"Hold on, Sugarplum!" Karl shouted over the rush. "Paddle, Cristina! Paddle hard!"

All they needed to do was to keep four or five feet off the bank, which would allow them to avoid the snags, sweepers, and deadfall.

"That's it! That's it!" he shouted. "We've got it knocked!"

Then suddenly Cristina stopped paddling and turned around.

"We're going to crash!" she cried.

"Not if we paddle!" Karl shouted. But it was too late.

Cristina turned forward again in time to duck, but Betty froze. Karl watched helplessly as a thick, crooked limb snatched her by the shirt and pulled her from the canoe.

"Daddy!" she cried as she went over the side.

Cristina looked back. She seemed to be screaming, but Karl could not hear her over the sound of the water. He leaned out and dug into the current with all his strength until finally he heard the grind of gravel against the bottom.

Only then did he permit himself to look at Betty, tiny and helpless against the headlong force of the river. He leaped out of the beached canoe and splashed madly in her direction, his strides shortening as the water got deeper and deeper.

Betty was holding herself just above the water, clinging to branches that jutted out just upstream from a deadly snag. The current helped by pushing her into the jutting limbs, though in the turbulence they trembled as if at any moment they might give way. She watched him moving upriver parallel to her. When he got above her field of vision, she tried to turn.

"I'm here, Betty!" he shouted. "Don't look for me! I'm here!"

The current pushed at him so hard that he had to put himself sideways so as to give it only his body's edge. He slid one foot, a baby step, then the other. The buoyant water made him light on the river bottom. The forces were in such delicate balance that so much as a doubt might have been enough to carry him away.

At some point he realized that he was not going to be able to reach her by wading. He stopped, looked down to where Cristina sat in the canoe, her face in her hands. He jumped.

In an instant he had Betty. The current pulled his legs downriver, curling him under her, until with a terrible crack the tree limb broke and they were both swept helplessly downriver.

His head went underwater, but he managed to kick away from the snag and hold her up above the maelstrom. Soon he was able to lie back, Betty on his belly, squirming but secure in his grip. His head came up and he gulped air. Then it went under again and he surrendered until the force of the water began to ease and he could let his feet down and find the bottom.

He stood, lifting her in his arms and carrying her to the middle of the river, where the gravel rose. He knew Cristina would never want to come to this place again. But he did not feel close to death. He felt that he was close to the truth of his life.

14

THE WORST PART OF OUR REVERSAL OF fortune was not that I had to adapt to it myself. My father had worked in the radio business, which had never given him much in the way of money, even when he served as the replacement man on the early-morning farm report. More than once an old gentleman in Abbeville told him that he brought the market to the town just as Grampa once had with his telegraph. I imagine that people wondered why such an obviously important man as my father drove such a rattletrap car.

So I knew I could make do with little. It was the effect on Julie and Rob that tore me apart. Even if I were to recover all our wealth and more tomorrow, I did not believe it would compensate for having to tell Rob that he would need to change schools.

"You can't do this to me," he said.

"New Trier is a fine institution," I said. "One of the best in the whole country. Everybody says so."

"I'll be a nobody there," he said, "just like I was before I transferred to Country Day."

"That's just not true, son," I said, though his crushing feeling of inadequacy had been the reason Julie and I had decided when he was in the fifth grade to transfer him out of public school.

"I know those kids," he said. "They'll make me into a big joke."

"You might be surprised at how much you've grown," I said. "You are a different young man now than when you left public school."

"What am I good at?" he said. "Name one thing."

"You are a good person," I said. "Start there."

Rob looked at me as if I had confirmed the worst.

"The world needs all different kinds of people," I said. "Not everyone has to be a star athlete or all-A student."

"But everybody needs to be somebody," he said, "which I am not, Dad. Let's face it."

He saw that I recognized the reference and almost smiled.

"Nobody knows more about movies than you do," I said. "I've heard you recite whole scenes from *It's a Wonderful Life* for your grandmother."

We had encouraged him many times to do something with this gift. But he was terrified when we took him to the Piven acting school. He did not even last the first session. He was a strong swimmer who had qualified as a lifeguard. But he grew so self-conscious about his body that he would not try out for the swim team, let alone think about pursuing a job at the beach, where some pretty young girl might have taught him about himself the way Julie had taught me.

Then there were the music lessons, the terrible struggle to get him to dance class, where we had foolishly hoped he might learn to loosen up a little. At some point I began to think he was in agony over homosexual feelings. When I finally dared to mention this to Julie, she laughed.

"You haven't seen the magazines he keeps under his mattress," she said.

Lately, though, it was more than dirty magazines she was finding there.

"He's smoking marijuana," she said.

"Can you imagine anyone doing that?" I said.

"That was different," she said. "It was never going to take over our lives. We had each other. But we know people who got hurt by it. They were the ones who were feeding an emptiness, the way Rob is."

"I'll talk to him," I said.

Though it was awkward, I did.

"Look," he said, "for a few minutes it makes me feel good, that's all. You've got to know what I'm talking about. I mean, the '60s and everything. It's no big deal."

"Your mother is concerned," I said.

"I'll be a lot more careful," he said.

My fear was that the transfer in the fall would push him toward something stronger.

"If New Trier doesn't work out," I said, "we'll move."

The fact was that we might have to anyway, to monetize some of the equity in our home and step way down on the mortgage.

"Is that supposed to make me feel better?" he said. "That I'm so lame that we may have to get out of town?"

"That you're so loved that we will do anything for you," I said.

"Anything but keep me in Country Day," he said.

"Anything we're able to do," I said. "I'm sorry, but I seem to have dragged us all down. I feel terrible about it."

"Join the club," he said.

I kept going in to Bishop & Dodge every day. I don't know why. Conference rooms that before the bubble burst had been booked weeks in advance now stood empty. A residue of disillusionment had settled over the board tables like dust. You could have written your name with your finger. But you didn't have to. The disaster already had everyone's name on it.

Some of my partners didn't even come in to the office anymore, preferring to count their losses in swizzle sticks lined up along a bar. Others hustled in early each morning as if they were still in a hurry and stayed late into the night because they simply did not know how not to.

The only part of the enterprise that remained busy was the law department, where one day I was summoned. There men and women waited on the reception couch and chairs. Others stood reading grim business magazines or staring blankly at the Bloomberg as it blinked away the tears. Oddest of all, people had begun to wear suits and ties and white shirts again. Business casual was history. It was as if, with all the starch taken out of a man's soul, he needed to have cladding in the cloth.

Solly Goldman's secretary appeared in the waiting area and nodded to me. I followed her to where the lawyer sat behind an enormous stack of documents.

"Pretty imposing," I said.

"If we get five cents on the dollar for any of the shit you guys bought they should hang my portrait in the foyer," he said. "Meanwhile lawsuits are flying around like bullets."

"Shooting the wounded," I said.

He stood and pointed me to the only two chairs that were unencumbered by paper.

"I don't know how to start, George," Goldman said. "We've been neighbors how long?"

"At the office a decade," I said. "In Wilmette even longer."

"It may seem funny coming from an attorney," he said, "but I basically believe in staying out of other people's business."

"Am I in trouble, Solly?" I said. "Is one of those bullets heading my way?"

Goldman shifted in his chair.

"This is strictly personal," he said. "I talked it over with Ginny for a long time last night because I wasn't sure. It's about Rob."

He breathed out, and I breathed in.

"He's been having issues," I said.

"Don't tell him this," he said, "but Erin told me certain things that he said to her. I don't know whether to believe them. Kids can exaggerate so."

"We already know about the marijuana," I said. "I won't incriminate myself, but I have my reasons not to be all that bothered."

"Erin told me you were going to pull him from the school," he said.

"I don't know what else to do," I said. "I don't have any cushion. The firm doesn't need me the way it does you, so I don't get any draw."

Goldman was looking at me but not seeing anything. I was sorry I had gotten into money troubles. Everybody had those.

"I guess I decided that if Rob told you that Erin had spoken to him about hurting herself, I would want to know," Goldman said.

He looked away. It took me a moment before I understood what he was telling me.

"What exactly did she tell you?" I said.

"Like I said, it's hard to know how serious anything is at this age," he said. "But if I held it in and something happened to Rob, I would never forgive myself."

"Did she say how it came up?" I said.

"They won't give you a straight answer, you know," he said. "They'll dance around everything that is important, then give you a blow-by-blow about how some girl dissed them in the lunch line."

"Solly," I pleaded.

"She said he told her yesterday that sometimes he thinks everybody would be better off if he were dead," Goldman said.

I heard the words, but I had a hard time connecting them to my son. I could not imagine what our lives would be worth if Rob took his. Suddenly I found myself in tears.

"I'm sorry," I said, standing to leave.

"You're going to need help, George," he said. "Listen to me because I know. I haven't told anybody else, but with Erin it was bulimia. Luckily we caught it early. You can beat this thing, George. Just don't be proud and try to go it alone."

"There's not much chance of pride," I said.

When I returned to my office, all I could do was sit at my desk and stare out the window at the empty sky. I had no idea how to reach Rob. I would, of course, insist that he see someone, but I couldn't make him open up or recognize his worth any more than I could make the Bloomberg swing from red to blue.

"Mr. Bailey?"

I looked up and saw the receptionist in the doorway. Now that we had let all the secretaries go, she was handling everyone's phone.

"Your wife is on the line," she said.

I wasn't ready to talk to Julie yet.

"I'll call her back," I said.

"She said it was urgent," the receptionist said. "It's not my place, but I think you'd better pick up the phone."

When I did, she turned and left. I didn't even have a chance to say hello before Julie started in.

"I just don't know what to do anymore," she said.

"I know the feeling," I said.

"The school just called," she said. "Rob never showed up for class this morning. I don't get it. This is the school where he wants desperately to stay."

"I'll come right home," I said. "I'll find him."

"You probably have other things," she said. "We can deal with this tonight."

"I don't think so," I said.

I had made the drive north thousands of times, usually crawling up the Kennedy and Edens Expressways in the rush-hour snarl. Now at midday I was able to keep the speedometer at sixty nearly the whole way. As the billboards and warehouses of the city yielded to the lawns and trees of the suburbs, I asked myself over and over again: When a little boy is so totally lost, how can his father hope to find him?

First I drove to the school. Even on the North Shore, where so little changed over the generations and social rank was handed down like a title of nobility, Country Day was a place out of time. It always made me think of what Chautauqua must have been like. I got out of the car and walked the empty grounds. But I knew; Rob would not have hovered.

I cruised the streets of Wilmette in lengthening radii from Green Bay Road, looking, looking. Even if Rob had been nearby he would have hidden the moment he saw the car. After a couple hours of searching, I drove to Gilson Park along the beach. There I parked and gazed out over the fathomless gray lake.

I don't know how long I had been there when in my peripheral vision I detected movement. I turned and saw a shadow walking in the distance among the trees. As it came closer, I told myself not to be foolish; it wasn't him. And yet the gait was familiar, the defeated slouch. He emerged from the trees a hundred yards from the car. I prayed he would not see me and bolt.

He stepped up onto the rocks at the edge of the lake. This was not the place he would choose to end his life, was it? He was too much of a swimmer. He stood motionless, giving no hint of his intention or even whether he had enough emotional energy to have one, just staring out over the rolling waves.

When I got out of the car, I was careful not to make any noise the waves would not cover. I circled back into the trees and came up to

Rob from behind. When I was ten feet away, I scuffed my feet a couple of times so as not to startle him. He turned, and a look of panic pulled at his face. He spun away from me back toward the lake.

"Don't, son," I said.

"What are you doing here?" he said to the water.

"Looking for answers," I said, "same as you."

He turned to me with a different face. It was exasperation, and I welcomed it.

"Who says that's what I'm doing?" he said.

"Why else do people come to the beach when it's too cold to swim?" I said.

"You know about school, don't you," he said.

"You must have realized they would call," I said.

"I'm really fucking up big time here," he said.

"You're not going to hear that from me," I said. "There's trouble all over. We're both trying to find our way through it."

"It isn't the same," he said.

"Don't you think I know that?" I said. "I didn't have me as a father, and you don't have me as a son. We're different people. But that doesn't mean we can't try to help each other."

I thought for a moment that he was going to come forward. Everything in me wanted to take him in my arms the way I had done when he was little and crying afraid. But he did not move.

"I'll take a ride home," he said.

15

WHEN THE MARKET CRASHED IN 1929, Abbeville barely noticed. The crops had all been harvested and, through Karl's magic, paid for. The proceeds were safe in Karl's bank. The only stock anyone owned ate feed and shat.

As winter came on, though, folks started to talk. The news in the *Trib* kept getting grimmer. President Hoover was talking about balancing the budget as a way out of the Panic. Congress was slapping tariffs on foreign products, and Europe was responding in kind against American grain.

Banks failed in Chicago, then in Kankakee. The farmers planted in the spring, even though prices were so low that some said it might be smarter to rest the land a year. Then the prices fell even further, and Karl's magic lost its power. Deposits dried up. Requests for credit increased. Farmers would have defaulted on loans if Karl hadn't extended terms. To be able to do this, he had to start sending excuses in lieu of payment to his corresponding banks.

Still, Karl as much as possible kept doing business as usual. His uncle had taught him to stand firm and wait for the tide to turn. After all, Karl was a man of substance; his credit was still good. He kept up appearances, kept bringing new implements onto the lot, because the antidote to panic was confidence.

"This thing will turn around," he said, "like they always have before."

Fritz came to him tapped out. He was going to lose everything if he couldn't get his hands on some cash fast. Karl looked at his brother for a moment, then went to the vault.

"Don't I need to sign something?" Fritz asked as Karl handed him the money.

"You're my brother," Karl said.

Despite the burden of his own debt, he walked across the prairie to work every morning as jauntily as if he had something to gain from it. Then one day just before breakfast Cristina called to him from the parlor. Across the tracks it looked as if all of Abbeville was lined up at the bank.

"What are you going to do?" she said.

"I'm going to finish my breakfast and coffee," he said. "Then I'm going to give you a kiss."

"Is there enough money for all of them?" she asked.

"I'll stop by Rose's," he said. "I think she's fallen ill."

"Why, I saw her at the church just last night," said Cristina. "She was fine."

"She deserves some time off," he said.

Betty, home from boarding school on a break, came down the stairs.

"Did you say Mrs. Stroeger is ill?" she said. "Should I bake her a cake?"

"You can't take on the whole Panic, Karl," said Cristina.

He buttered his toast and used it to push the last of the scrambled eggs onto his fork.

"I'm mighty slow at counting money," he said. "You've seen me. One bill at a time."

"It will take forever," Cristina said.

"That it will," said Karl.

He appeared at the bank a few minutes before opening time, wearing his newest suit. Cristina went with him, carrying in one hand a basket containing every cinnamon bun they had found in the store. From the other swung a canister of coffee to keep everyone warm.

"It will make them able to wait longer," she said when he told her how to prepare.

"It will show that we're not afraid of their waiting," he said.

When he reached the bank, the crowd at the door parted.

"Looks like opening day at the county fair," Karl said.

"You know why we're here," said Robert Schlagel, who was in arrears three months on the debit side for a tractor. What he had on deposit wouldn't have paid for much more than the cinnamon buns.

"We hate to have to do it," said George Loeb. He looked as if he might weep.

Karl took each customer inside, one by one. Cristina waited outside as the crowd strained to look through the windows to see what was happening. Small talk was difficult, but she tried. Occasionally peals of laughter would come from inside and a minute later a customer would emerge, grinning over the thin fold of greenbacks in his hand.

"He's a good one, all right. I have half a mind to give this back," said Will Hoenig.

"Nobody's ever accused you of having half a mind, Will," said Bernard Lampere.

"Go ahead, Hoenig," said Prideaux. "It will just mean more for us."

"You can have mine, too, Prideaux," said old Henry Mueller. "I'm leaving."

The day wore on. The buns and coffee ran out. Karl took longer and longer with each customer. The crowd became surly and grew in number. People from all over Cobb County had heard that they had better hightail it to Abbeville or risk losing everything.

"There ain't enough to go around, you watch," said Prideaux. "That's why he's dawdling so. Remember, everybody, I warned you."

Suddenly Harley Ansel pushed his way to the front of the line, all the authority of the law behind him. He had kept a stake in Karl's bank, and Karl had always wondered why. The county prosecutor entered the door as Robert Hesse came out empty-handed.

"I let it ride," Hesse said. "For all Karl has done, it's the least we can do."

Ansel looked over his shoulder at Hesse as he said it and shook his head. Within a matter of minutes he was back outside.

"The bank's busted," he shouted.

"You busted it," said Hesse.

Karl came to the door as the prosecutor strode away.

"Thank you for your patience," he said. "But Harley is right."

"He's going to have something more to say about all this," said Hesse.

"Yes," said Karl, "I suppose he will."

16

To GET TO CHICAGO KARL HOPPED A FREIGHT that had stopped in Abbeville to switch two empty boxcars onto the siding next to the elevator. In the past he had always flagged down a streamliner. But that was when he could pay.

He climbed into a boxcar and slid its door nearly shut. The last time he had ridden this way had been leaving Verdun. The train began to move. Click-click. A cold draft came through the planking, but here there was no stench of the trenches to blow away. The smell was not mankind's shame but earth's pride: good, golden grain.

The only shame in the boxcar was Karl's own. He sat down and drew his knees up to conserve the warmth that was still in his belly from the big breakfast Cristina had set out for him when he had come upstairs from stoking the furnace. Next to him he placed the sack that held the sandwich she had made for his lunch and an old jar full of apple juice she had pressed in the summer. As for sustenance for what might be a night on the streets of Chicago, Karl could only hope he could prevail on Uncle John for some change.

But it wasn't money he had come for. At first he had even hesitated to write and ask for an audience. What he was looking for was an idea, a strategy, an approach, anything to push against the gravity that was pulling down everything around him. He was not sure he would be able to explain this to Uncle John. But in the end embarrassment was just one more luxury he could no longer afford, and so he sent the letter. It took five weeks before he received a reply. "I will entertain a visit," was all Uncle John had written.

Meanwhile, Harley Ansel had surfaced with a pocketful of subpoenas.

"He's not my kin anymore," said Ansel's uncle, Henry Mueller. "He should be talking to all the men you carried on your back. It's a wonder you haven't broken it."

At times Karl did ache under the weight. He shifted his position on the boxcar floor and felt the icy stiffness in his hips and knees. He was too old for trouble.

"You saved everybody's money," Cristina said one blue night at the dinner table.

It was true, as far as it went. He had found a buyer for all the bank's assets but the building. The bargain he drove held the depositors harmless. In return, he did not take a penny out of the deal.

"I have not paid my debts," he told Cristina. "The banks that lent to me lost everything but what they might salvage from a pauper's auction."

"Just like you lost everything lending to the farmers," she said. "And to Fritz."

"The farmers couldn't help it," Karl said.

"Nor could a man as good and steady and competent as Karl Schumpeter," Cristina said.

But he could have been more careful. He had believed in being bold. He had believed he could modernize Abbeville and protect it. He had believed that what conquered adversity was confidence. Confidence. Now he knew why they used that word for a swindle.

The boxcar shook as the engine began to brake. Karl crawled to the door against the momentum and looked furtively through the opening. They were still in the middle of farm country. In the distance the two familiar church steeples reached upward to a place beyond fear that no living being had ever inhabited.

At least there was no danger of railroad detectives here, even if the train came to a stop, which in the end it did not do. Soon the engine began to accelerate again, adding to Karl's weight as he pulled himself back deeper into his corner.

Harley Ansel did not approach Karl directly. Karl only heard that something was up from a friend at the Bank of Potawatomi, with which he had made the deal. His friend told him that Ansel had subpoenaed the records of the sale along with all the files and ledgers that had gone with it.

"You'd better get a lawyer, Karl," Cristina had said.

"And pay for it with what?" Karl said. "Corncobs?"

Instead he simply waited, going every day to the abandoned bank, passing the rusting dynamo in the shack with its stove-in roof, waiting for Harley Ansel to come. Months passed with no activity. An eerie calm fell over the town, everybody keeping to themselves because it was no use telling your troubles to someone with as many as you. The house was quiet, too, with Betty away at high school, earning her way by keeping house for the folks who owned the paper in Potawatomi. Karl and Cristina sat at the dinner table every evening until it was time to go to bed. Sometimes neither said a word.

The train ticked along steadily now, and the draft made Karl draw his overcoat tighter around his suit and pull up over his ears the wool

scarf Cristina had knitted him out of remnants she had found in drawers in the attic warming the mice. He looked down at the shoes he had
bought years before at the Fair Store, beautiful hand-tooled leather,
now cracked. Shining them the night before, he had thought of what
an odd hobo he was, half-looking like he was going to dinner on the
Gold Coast.

Well, you got used to contrasts these days: women working, their
men idle; farmers unsure their harvest would fetch enough to cover
the cost of the seed; Fritz's roads so broken and overgrown they seemed
like trails left behind by the Indians.

Cristina had been a strength to Karl throughout the trouble. She
would simply not hear him talk of failure. She always brought him
back to what endured: faith, love, their daughter, the friendship of
their neighbors.

"Would you trade those to get the money back?" she asked.

"I guess I never thought we would have to," Karl said.

"Occasionally," she said, "a man can be wrong about the weather."

The second winter after the Crash brought heavy snows, which
made folks' isolation almost complete. Betty could not get home. Karl
even stopped going to the bank each morning. At church only a scat-
tering of parishioners listened in the pews as the preacher told the
story of Job. When hymn time came, Karl's monotone so dominated
that it threw off the organist. So instead of four-part German har-
mony lifting everyone beyond Job's suffering, the song limped to a
close like a broken soul.

With the thaw, Otter Creek flooded. In the interest of his creditors
Karl shored up the high-side bank with old railroad ties so the road to
his cabin would not collapse. The process by which his debts would
finally consume cabin, house, and other worldly goods moved as
slowly as Ansel did. The system was so clogged with rotten loans
that when institutional creditors looked at what Karl had left and

what they could get for it, they put the file at the bottom of the in-box.

Through the door of the boxcar farmland was giving way to city. Karl hoped the train would push straight into the hub and not beach itself in some remote switchyard, where he would have to avoid the railroad dicks and hitch a ride downtown.

There was always a Samaritan ready to give a stranger a hand. In fact the hard times seemed to make folks more giving. Rose Stroeger had trudged through the snowdrifts one day to deliver Karl and Cristina a casserole she claimed she would never be able to finish herself. Old Henry Mueller showed up another day with a load of cobs he pretended he needed to dispose of. And when the gypsies came through, Cristina always found some little bit of food to give them.

Then there was Fritz. To outward appearances he was holding up better than anyone else. Karl was glad that Betty hadn't been there the day he'd shown up at the house, because she blamed him for everything. Karl supposed it was natural. When you are young you want to think that bad things happen because of bad people, which is easier to bear than the fact that they just simply happen, like God's snow bringing down the roof of a barn. Nor did she understand, because they had been unable to give her a sibling, how the instinct to resent could yield to the urge to protect.

"To what do I owe the honor?" Karl said, rising from his rocker as Fritz let himself in.

Fritz pulled off his boots and put them on some papers Cristina had left at the door for the purpose. Then he unwound himself from a muffler and heavy coat that looked as soft as cashmere.

"A brother needs a reason?" said Fritz.

"Of course not," said Karl. "But he usually has one."

Fritz bellowed with laughter, which brought Cristina into the room. She said hello, smiled, and left.

"Well, you got me there, Karl," Fritz said. "Here. I brought you a decent cigar to chew on."

He handed it to Karl, who rolled it between his thumb and fingers as carefully as if it were an ancient artifact.

"Don't ask who I got it from," Fritz said.

Karl put the cigar down on the marble-topped humidor next to his rocker.

"Go ahead and enjoy it," Fritz said. "It's not going to incriminate you."

"You getting any business?" Karl said.

"It's starting to come," said Fritz. "That's what I wanted to talk to you about. Things happen when the money starts moving again."

"I'm not involved in that," said Karl. "For me the money has stopped cold. And whatever paper there was between us belongs to the State Bank of Potawatomi now."

"I've heard from them," Fritz said. "They're not the bankers you were."

"You mean they expect to be repaid," said Karl.

"I've heard from Harley Ansel, too," said Fritz.

Karl rocked in his chair a few times, then lifted the cigar off the humidor and held it out to Fritz.

"It is better that this stay between you and him," Karl said.

Fritz made no move to accept its return.

"Harley's never given me anything but trouble," Fritz said.

Karl put the cigar back down.

"There was a time you thought you could get on his good side," he said. "You gave him one of Father's fancy pony bridles once, remember? You got a whooping for it."

"I don't know why Father put up such a fuss," said Fritz. "We didn't have any ponies anymore."

"Maybe because he knew that tribute would only make Harley demand more," said Karl.

"You ended up having to fight him, as I recall," Fritz said. "And then Father whooped you for bloodying your shirt."

"He didn't have much use for the argument that I was defending the family honor," Karl said.

"'If you always do the right thing,'" Fritz said, imitating their father's accent, "'the family honor will be strong enough not to need to hide behind your fists.'"

Karl pulled the wrapper off the cigar, leaving on the ring, and put the uncut end in his mouth. It had been a long time since he had held such richness between his lips. The leaves were dark and strong, and a pleasant feeling went straight to his head.

"What would Father say now, eh?" Karl said.

Fritz's eyes dropped to the paper Karl had on the floor to catch the juice he spit out.

"I'm the one he would say it to, Fritz," Karl said, "not you."

"Ansel has subpoenaed my business records," Fritz said. "He's building a case."

"What kind of a case?" Karl said.

The tobacco suddenly had an edge.

"It could be any number of things," Fritz said. His left hand with the heavy wedding band on it worked his right, as if they ached from actual exertion.

It would have been better, Karl thought, if they had both stuck to the farmer's life their father had envisioned for them. Family honor had its most secure residence in black dirt beneath fingernails.

"Maybe we'd better be careful what we talk about here," Karl said. "If we're not, he'll have me on the witness stand against you."

"It's the other way around."

And as soon as Fritz said it, Karl knew that it had to be so. He rocked back and forth.

"He says he'll go easy on me if I testify against you," Fritz said.

Karl looked at him and saw a rabbit ready to run.

"Testify to what?" he said.

"About the bank," said Fritz.

"He already has all the records of the bank," said Karl.

"Not the loans you didn't record," said Fritz.

Karl kept rocking. The floorboard beneath him sounded off under his weight. Tick-tick.

"He says I'm going to jail one way or another," Fritz said. "It's only a matter of how long."

"You won't go to jail, Fritz," Karl said.

"Harley Ansel is a vicious man," said Fritz.

"You won't go to jail."

The sun directly overhead had warmed the boxcar enough that Karl could open his coat. He pulled his watch from his vest pocket and saw that it was lunchtime, so he unwrapped the sandwich and followed it with a juicy apple that Cristina had polished to a warm red glow. For an instant he felt like a rich man, because even when he was a rich man he had never gotten as much pleasure from an apple.

The engine began to brake heavily. Karl stood, bracing himself against the planking, and made his way again to the sliding door. The train was already in the city. It rolled past great gray factories, past gigantic grain elevators that Karl had once been strong enough to tame. He smelled the stockyards. The train was very near the main rail yard now. He could ride all the way in, but then he would run a great risk of being arrested by the railroad dicks. So he gathered up his things and pushed the door open as the train swayed slowly over some switches.

He sat in the doorway, then jumped. When he hit the ballast, his feet slid out from under him and he found himself rolling. The bed of clinkers where he came to a stop was made to steady the rails, not to comfort a human body. When he stood, he saw that he had ripped out one knee of his pants, which already showed the dampness of blood. It was just a scrape. He tore off a corner of his lunch bag and wiped away what he could. Cristina would be able to repair the fabric adequately, and the stain would come out well enough. But at this moment he felt more like a man who was coming apart than one who was on his way to a center of high finance.

At the road his luck changed, and the second car slowed for his thumb.

"You have a flat or something?" asked the driver, who wore the coveralls of someone who worked with machines. "I didn't see your car back there."

"Don't have one anymore," said Karl.

"Man like you usually does," said the driver.

"I came by freight," said Karl. "That's the kind of man I am."

"Well, this mess don't respect class much, does it," said the driver. "Least I have a job, praise God."

"I praise God for it, too," said Karl.

The driver turned and looked at him.

"Otherwise," Karl said, "you wouldn't have a car either, and I'd still be walking down the side of this road."

"Now that is a healthy attitude," the driver said.

He generously delivered Karl directly to the Rookery Building, where Uncle John still had his office.

"Thank you kindly," said Karl.

"Keep your chin up, brother," said the driver.

Nothing had changed upstairs but the receptionist behind the glass. She was about the same age Luella had been when Karl had first come out of the woods. She looked Karl up and down until he said his name. Then she raised a penciled eyebrow, plugged a line into the switchboard, and said simply, "Well, he's here."

Before Karl sat down, the door opened.

"You can come in," the receptionist said. "He says you know the way."

"I worked here once," Karl said.

"A lot of people used to," she said.

As he moved down the corridor, two of every three offices were vacant. He wondered whether Uncle John might let him sleep in one of them tonight.

"Come in," Uncle John said when Karl knocked on the burnished wood door frame at the end of the hall.

Karl moved forward and put out his hand. Uncle John stood but kept the desk between them.

"Sit. Sit," he said.

Karl was relieved to be able to hide his torn knee beneath the rim of the desk.

"Thank you for seeing me," he said.

"It has been too long," said Uncle John, looking somewhere else.

"I don't have any business to offer you," Karl said.

"I'm sorry the investments you had with us did not work out," said Uncle John, "but in this you are in excellent company."

"Your business survives," Karl said.

"Barely, as you can see," said Uncle John bitterly. "My losses have been staggering. But fortunately, people still need to eat, so the promise of grain is still bought and sold, though at a much reduced rate."

Karl shifted uncomfortably in his chair, which seemed designed to bite into his back.

"I came for advice," he said.

He was prepared to meet his uncle's eyes, but Uncle John was still not ready to meet his.

"Risk is a medicine like mercury that in the wrong dosage kills," said Uncle John. "But my advice is the same as it always has been. Move against the current."

Karl leaned forward until his hands touched the front edge of the desk.

"I am drowning," he said.

"I sincerely hope you put by some seed corn over the winter," Uncle John said.

"How could I have done that?" Karl said. "Everything was swept away."

"Only gold has sufficient weight to anchor itself," Uncle John said.

"Gold?" said Karl. "But what about the creditors?"

"That is what attorneys are for," said Uncle John, "to study ancient texts like kabbalists and find incantations that make dense gold invisible."

"I used whatever magic I had in me to protect the people who trusted me," said Karl.

The look on Uncle John's face was the one he gave to loggers and secretaries, the face with which success always gazes upon failure.

"Someday perhaps you will learn not to dissipate your strength," he said. "Spread it, and it withers. Keep it for yourself alone, and it can be preserved. Do you ever see that girl I fired?"

"Occasionally," Karl said. "For a cup of coffee."

"It is all right to sip the coffee now," said Uncle John. "You are married. And in need of stimulant."

"It is nothing like that," said Karl, standing. He would not ask for a place to sleep. Not even for the coins it would take to get a meal.

"If you go to her," Uncle John said, "do remember about the mercury."

As he left the building, he wondered why he had ever thought Uncle John would have anything worthwhile to tell him. He walked what felt like miles toward the place where Luella worked, punishing himself the whole distance for imagining that the conversation with his uncle would turn out well. But when he drew near, his spirits lifted. He hadn't seen Luella since everything had fallen apart, and he hoped it might be easier now to be friends. Perhaps she would not feel obliged to lecture him on the rise of the proletariat and they could talk about important things.

When he reached the building, the sign of the realty firm still hung out over the sidewalk, but the windows were boarded up. Next door a cobbler was at work saving shoes that in other times would have gone into the trash.

"Do you know where Southwest Real Estate moved to?" Karl asked.

The cobbler took the nails from his mouth and set them on his bench.

"Same place the car dealer did a few months before," he said. "Busted Boulevard."

"What about Luella Grundy?" Karl asked. "A redheaded woman. You couldn't have missed her."

"Oh, I miss her, all right," the cobbler said. "Seeing her coming and going was the light of my day. She went somewhere with that lucky fella of hers."

"You wouldn't know where," said Karl.

The cobbler picked up the nails.

"Nowadays people vanish, like everything else," he said.

17

THE DOOR OF THE VAULT SEEMED HEAVIER this evening as Karl put his shoulder into it. Locking the safe was a daily ritual, even though the cash was long gone. He went to his desk, which was no longer cluttered. The lights flickered, the way they had back in the days of the dynamo. Why had he ever thought he could chase away darkness, even from this one small place? Always at the end of the day comes night. And in the end of the ends, it takes you with it.

The building stayed lighted now only because it fell under the protection of the bankruptcy court. The notice of auction had finally appeared. Everything would go under the gavel within a month. He would not be there to see it, but he had assurances that no one would be bidding against Fred Krull for the house and its contents, and Krull promised to rent it to the family for a dollar a month until, little by little, Betty was able to buy it back.

It hardly seemed possible that so much time had passed—the good years when business boomed and Karl kept his promises, then the terrible fall, how it compounded on the way down faster than it had on the way up. Then did not stop.

"What do you want from me?" Karl had asked point-blank in Ansel's office in Potawatomi.

"What do you have to offer?" Ansel replied, not even deigning to stop arranging and rearranging the things on his meticulous desk.

"I know what I want," Karl said.

"We've all had unrequited desires," said Ansel.

"I need you to understand one thing first," Karl said. "You had no right to claim Cristina. It was her life, not her father's or yours or mine."

"But she got yours, didn't she," Ansel said. "For better or for worse."

"Fritz goes free," Karl said.

"That will cost you," said Ansel, hands flitting from here to there as if he were tending a web.

"Whatever it takes," said Karl.

"Well then," said Ansel. "Let's get down to business."

And so later tonight Karl was leaving for the county jail to await transport to Stateville to serve a two-year sentence. He turned off the lights and locked the door behind him. The air outside was brittle. He had gone to the bank with his coat unbuttoned to take in the sunshine of the morning. Now it was winter dark, and as he stood at the door a chill went down to his belly.

The Coliseum was shuttered. Abbeville could have used a little high-kicking fiddle music right now. You could probably get somebody to play for pennies. But who had pennies? Karl stopped and looked into the window of the general store that he had sold to Will Hoenig. The new owner sat in his white apron on a pile of empty wooden Coca-Cola crates, blood from the butcher block dried brown at his waist, one hand rubbing the other. The chill of the meat locker had always made Karl's hands stiffen, too. He squeezed his right hand into a fist and shivered again. Even in the meat locker he had never felt like this.

He stepped back from the window and began moving toward the rail crossing again. Up ahead he could hear laughter. Someone had probably just misplayed a pinochle hand, and the others were letting him know it.

At the doorway of the garage, Karl stopped and looked in. Fred Brock was dealing. They all turned except Brock, who finished flipping the cards then squared the deck. Now that Karl had been seen, it wouldn't be right just to slink away. He opened the door and took one step inside to face them.

"Well," old Henry Mueller said, "are you just going to stand there like the Grim Reaper or do you have the guts to sit down and play?"

"You fellas look a mite too accomplished for me," Karl said.

"He looks like he's quaking in his boots, don't he?" said Will Trague, who had started the garage out of his blacksmith business with money from Karl's bank.

"We're playing for matchsticks," said George Loeb. "Pull up a chair. We need someone to be the banker."

The others suddenly started studying their cards.

"I've got chores up to the house," Karl said. "You know how it is."

"Be sure to tell Cristina that if she needs anything . . ." said Loeb.

"To call any of us," said Mueller.

It touched Karl that he could count on these men. But he wondered if it crossed Henry's mind, as it kept crossing his own, that Cristina would have been better off if she had stuck with Henry's nephew.

He left the garage and walked quickly toward the rail crossing, whose lights had just begun to flash. He pulled out his pocket watch. The moon was new, so he had to move closer to the crossing signal and hold the watch up to catch the red, blinking light. He felt the rumble of the train beneath his feet as his finger felt for the catch. In the distance he saw the train's swinging light. The watch's hands stood at 8:09. The freight was right on time.

He had talked to Cristina before going to Harley Ansel. He had laid out the alternatives, none of them good.

"It tears at me," he said, "but Harley will be able to send me away no matter what. Now all I can do is try not to pull anyone down with me."

"You do what's right, Karl," Cristina said. "That's all any man can do."

Across the tracks stood the church where Karl had prayed often for the dead German's soul. How many nights had he gone there to ask God for guidance? At first how to protect those who depended on him. Then later how to do the least harm. He stepped past the lowered counterweight of the crossing arm. The bells were sounding the two-note warning: *It's wrong. It's right. It's wrong. It's right.* The rail curved beneath his shoe as he stepped forward and looked south again. The ground shook, and the light on the engine flickered like a flare.

People had been hit at this crossing several times before. Kurt Handke had gotten his wagon stuck. The engine had hit behind him as he'd tried to pull loose, then dragged him and the horses back under the wheels of the tender, heavy with a fresh load of coal. Maude Goebel, whose husband had died a month before, had been late to church one Sunday and tried to beat the streamliner. Some whispered that she hadn't really tried.

The track beneath his foot began to pulse. Tick-tick. He stopped. *In this life God's grace is nothing you earn, nor is punishment the proof of sin. This is the first great mystery, and it is only made bearable by the second, which is love.* As he shifted his weight to move forward, his foot slipped. His shoe wedged itself between the rail and the planking of the crossing. He looked down the track. The light was closing in on him. The engineer blew the horn. It was as if the bobbing light had hypnotized him. He could not move. Then he looked away from it, reached down, found the lace, and pulled it. The power of the train sucked all the breath from him as he fell.

The next thing he knew he was lying on the ground, one foot shoeless, as a hundred freight cars passed.

When the caboose rolled by, one of the trainmen was looking out the window. Karl picked himself up and waved so the man would not be alarmed. The shoe now was nothing more than a strip of torn hide. He pried it loose from the rail.

The bells had stopped, but the sound of the train was still so full in his ears that he barely heard the voice behind him.

"Are you all right?"

It was Will Hoenig.

"I almost ended up on the cowcatcher," Karl said, limping a step in his direction.

"You need a hand walking?" Hoenig asked.

"God seems to want to keep me going," said Karl. "To what purpose is a question only He can answer."

"Anyone in Abbeville can answer that one, Karl," said Hoenig.

Karl hobbled away from him toward the house. At night you could not see that it had grown shabby for want of paint.

"Karl, what happened?" Cristina said, looking at his one bare foot, the dust all over him.

He took her in his arms and could feel her breath coming in sobs, though she was not letting herself make a sound. Maybe a man could only live if he didn't fight the forces that tossed him about. Maybe he could learn to love them as he was supposed to love God.

"I'm so afraid," Cristina said as he pressed himself against her sorrow.

"I will be able to handle whatever comes," he said, "if I know you can."

And as he held her, he could actually feel them both giving in to the greater mystery.

"I guess I'd better get ready," he said.

"So soon?" she said.

She increased her hold on the whole length of him.

"I don't want anybody saying we couldn't face it," he said.

The sheriff arrived late. When he appeared at the door, Karl's valise was sitting outside, packed. The sheriff did not take off his wide-brimmed hat of natural straw or open his tan jacket. Around his waist hung a belt with a pistol and a pair of handcuffs in a leather case. He did not wear a star. He did not have to. Just by looking at him, anybody would know to respect this man's authority.

"Had a little trouble up to Milford," he said.

"It's all right, John," Karl said. "I've got nothing but time."

John Hawk had been an acquaintance of Karl's for years. He had succeeded Karl as Abbeville's sheriff when Karl had gone to France. Karl had spoken for him at several campaign events when Hawk had run for sheriff of all of Cobb County. That was back when Karl's endorsement had been something candidates wanted.

"Well, I guess it's time you come with me," Hawk said.

Karl took the old leather bag his father had gotten him mail order when he had sent him off to learn the ways of the world. It carried the marks of that journey and many others. Water spots, scuffs, a sticker from the World's Columbian Exposition.

As he passed the bureau in the foyer, he put his hand into the big old ceramic bowl that Cristina kept filled with sweets for him. He offered Hawk a stick of gum.

"That's mighty good of you, Karl," said Hawk.

"I'm still a Republican," said Karl, "even if I can't vote anymore."

Hawk went to the car first to let Karl make his farewell.

"Good-bye, my love," he said to Cristina. "Please forgive me."

Cristina held him.

"The one thing I will not be able to bear," she said, "is your being sorry."

"For abandoning you again," he said.

"Don't you think I can tell the difference between running off and being taken?" she said. "Go now and number the days. Each will be one less."

Karl started to leave, then turned and gave her hand one last touch—leaving in it the gold watch. After that he could not look back.

Outside, the sheriff had the car running. Karl opened the door and slipped in next to him. The heater was cranked up so high that Karl had to open his coat. Then he offered his wrists for the cuffs.

The sheriff barely glanced in Karl's direction as he shifted into gear, let out the clutch, and got the car rolling forward.

"Put your hands down, Karl," he said. "You're no criminal."

"I admitted to the judge that I am," said Karl.

He looked straight ahead through the windshield as the car swung onto the road out of Abbeville. The sheriff cleared his throat.

"A lot of folks feel as though they wouldn't've made it if you hadn't stretched for them," the sheriff said.

"Harley Ansel didn't charge me with aggravated helping," said Karl. "I made mistakes. I really thought I could ride it out and cover them."

"Then Harley should've charged you with being a damn fool," said the sheriff. "There's not room in Stateville for all of us that's been one of those."

Sheriff Hawk turned north at the corner, but when the highway curved east, he did not follow it.

"You missed the turn," said Karl.

"I ain't taking you to the county jail tonight," said Hawk, "if that's what you were thinking."

"It's trouble if I don't show up," said Karl.

The wheels under them spun on the unoiled gravel, one of the many corners Fritz had cut.

"You hungry?" asked Hawk.

"I hadn't even thought of it," said Karl.

"Gert'll be pretty upset if you don't at least make an effort," said Hawk.

"Gert packed me a meal?" said Karl.

"She's made a proper dinner, Karl," said the sheriff, "with all the fixings. You're going to stay the night with us. First thing in the morning I'll take you to meet the Stateville van."

Karl looked at him and did not know what to say.

"Tonight'll count against your sentence," said the sheriff, "so don't you go worrying about that."

18

WHEN I WOKE UP IN THE OLD HOUSE, I realized I had slept as I had not in months. I'm sure there were dreams, but I could not summon them. I had a quick breakfast and set out for Potawatomi.

The records of Grampa's trial turned out to be remarkably accessible. An elderly lady at the courthouse bade me sit and read the newspaper while she dispatched a young man to fetch them from the basement.

"I just hope the mice haven't gotten to them," she said.

The day's newspapers sat neatly scalloped on a big table that, though worn by what looked like a century of use, had obviously been polished that very morning. I could not help but contrast this with the few encounters I'd had with officialdom in the city. Once I'd had to make four separate trips to the Illinois Secretary of State's office to accomplish the simple transfer of the title of a car. That office resided in a monstrous state building not more than a decade old, yet it was already shabbier than the Potawatomi courthouse.

"Mr. Bailey?" said the woman. "Here's your material."

The file was not thick.

"You may not take it out of this room," she said. "But the desks over there are comfortable. If there is anything you would like to copy, it is seven cents a page, I'm afraid."

I thanked her and sat down. The papers inside were yellow and brittle with years, typed by hand on an old manual typewriter that registered the variable impact of the fingers in the density of ink on each letter. Though this gave the sheets an uneven appearance, I was amazed that there were no corrections. The typist must have had to start a whole page over if she made a mistake. The cost of error had been very high in those days.

I had hoped to find a grand jury transcript to learn what secret things Harley Ansel had said about Grampa. But beyond the indictment itself, there was no grand jury record in the file. The only hint came in the transcript of the sentencing hearing after Grampa's guilty plea:

JUDGE: Does the prosecution wish to make any statement?

PROSECUTOR: I draw Your Honor's attention to the checks the defendant drew on the Bank of Abbeville in the months after October 29 of 1929. Your Honor will find purchases of tailored clothing from Chicago and various other luxuries. I would draw your particular attention to the draft paid to one Hempstead & Strong, London, England. The accompanying invoice shows that this was in payment for a handmade bamboo fishing pole and brass reel.

DEFENDANT: rod.

JUDGE: You will have your opportunity to speak, Karl.

DEFENDANT: It was a fishing rod, not a fishing pole.

PROSECUTOR: I stand corrected, Your Honor. Obviously the purchase was even fancier than I had thought.

DEFENDANT: I had money in my account to cover those checks.

JUDGE: Karl, hush, now.

PROSECUTOR: Money you could have used to pay some of your debts.

JUDGE: If that is the reason for the prosecution's recommended sentence, I have a problem. A man spending his money unwisely is not a crime.

PROSECUTOR: It goes to the defendant's state of mind, Your Honor. He didn't give a damn.

JUDGE: Harley, you know better than to use that kind of language in my court.

I looked over the list of items in the transcript, and it was clear that Grampa was trying to continue a lifestyle that had become untenable. I felt the tug to do that myself every time I looked at Rob or Julie. To be honest, I also felt it when I saw a sharp new sports car pass me on the expressway, the kind you could hop into, put the top down, and flee.

JUDGE: Why did you do it, Karl?

DEFENDANT: I make no excuse.

JUDGE: But an explanation. Something.

DEFENDANT: At first I did not want to alarm my family. Then I wanted to show folks confidence. In the end I suppose I kept going just because I didn't know how to stop.

PROSECUTOR: The defendant has agreed not to contest the prosecution's recommended sentence.

JUDGE: It's mighty harsh, Harley.

DEFENDANT: I have my reasons, Your Honor.

JUDGE: I understand the guilty plea, Karl. Those loans you made off the books, well, there's no getting around them. But I've always known you to drive a pretty hard bargain, and two years' hard time looks like you got the worst deal you could.

DEFENDANT: I knew what I was doing, Tom. I mean, Your Honor.

JUDGE: It is going to be mighty hard on Cristina and your young daughter.

PROSECUTOR: Your Honor, this emotional display by the defendant is uncalled for.

JUDGE: For heaven's sake, Harley. Can't you even let the man weep?

Grampa never once hinted at the connection to Fritz.

When I had finished with the documents, I carefully returned them to the file and gave them back to the woman behind the desk.

"Did you find what you were looking for?" she asked.

WHEN IT HAD COME time for my mother to move into a retirement home, she chose one closer to Abbeville than to Park Forest. This made it a trek for me to visit her from Chicago, but she seemed to know everyone in Cobb County, so she did not want for company.

Today, though, the location was an advantage. The drive from Potawatomi only took twenty minutes. I had called ahead and told her I would be there shortly. She asked where I was, and I told her.

"You're coming from the wrong direction," she said.

"I stayed the night in Abbeville," I said.

"You did?" she said, obviously pleased. "It looks real good, doesn't it?"

The retirement home was a rambling, four-story structure with a colonial facade, set back from the road behind a broad lawn. My mother had a two-room apartment stuffed with every piece of furniture from her house that she could fit. It was a wonder she could get around it with her walker.

The door was ajar when I arrived. I knocked and went in.

"It's me," I said.

She labored to stand.

"Don't get up," I said.

"I want my hug," she said.

She had become quite frail after her stroke. I was careful when I embraced her, but she held on to me with surprising force.

"You did want a hug," I said.

"It's been a long time," she said.

"Only a few weeks," I said.

"It's been a year," she said.

"We're going to have to get a notebook I can sign each time I come so you'll remember," I said.

"I'd just forget to look at it," she said.

She never had any trouble remembering her years in Abbeville.

"Your grandma wrote him every day," she told me. "But he only replied once. 'Until I come home again pretend I don't exist,' he wrote. 'It will be easier that way.' So your grandma naturally decided that I should go."

"Were you afraid?" I asked.

"I went," my mother said.

WILL HOENIG DROVE HER in a truck that Karl had sold him. They bounced over roads that had deteriorated badly as the money dried up. This made the trip slow and uncomfortable.

"Your Uncle Fritz could have used a little more asphalt on this stretch," Mr. Hoenig said.

"Don't let's talk about him, all right?" said Betty.

She knew that people wanted to take her side, but they didn't know how dark her feelings were or they wouldn't have wanted to be anywhere near her.

"They say there's justice in the next world," Mr. Hoenig went on. "If there is, I hope it puts Fritz on roads like this for all eternity."

It took hours to get to Joliet. Mr. Hoenig had to tack back and forth to avoid the potholes, and he did not always succeed. He fixed two flat tires along the way. It reminded Betty of the time they had driven to Michigan, which made her think of drowning.

The prison, with its limestone walls and battlements, seemed to have come down from the time of dragons. A low building that looked incongruously like a home stood at the gate. Several families had already queued up at the door. A meaty matron in a blue coat with a badge and black Sam Browne belt sat behind a small table reading a crime magazine.

"Will I be able to see my father today?" Betty asked her.

"What did you say, girl?" said the matron. "Speak up."

"My father is in this jail," Betty said, forcing herself to stand proud.

"It's up to him if he wants to see you," said the matron, who took her name and passed her on to another, thinner matron who led her down a long corridor. A heavy door closed behind them with such a clang that Betty thought it might never open again.

Eventually they reached a room deep in the interior. In it sat rows of straight-backed benches. There were also a number of heavy chairs. She took one of them and scraped it along the stone toward a solitary corner.

A dozen other people were waiting in the room, women mostly, looking tired. All except one, that is. She had exuberantly red hair and a bright light behind her eyes. Her skirt billowed—old-country style—as if she were an actress in a play. Betty wondered what remarkable kind of man she was visiting. A gypsy king, perhaps. Or somebody the *Tribune* would call an anarchist.

From time to time the matron presiding over the room called a name. Finally it was Betty's.

"I hope you aren't planning to take that inside," said the matron, pointing to the sack in Betty's hand. Cristina had given it to her full of Karl's favorites. It had become oily in several places from the short-ening, so you could almost see right through the paper. The matron took it away from her.

"That's for my father," Betty protested. "Harley Ansel said he cheated his own bank, but he never cheated anybody in his whole life."

"I lost all my money in a bank," said the matron. She turned some pages on a clipboard, putting her finger to the lists. "Karl Schumpeter must be quite a fellow, because you're the second female here to see him today. The other's a regular, but I don't know you."

"I'm his daughter," said Betty. "His only daughter."

The matron wrote it down.

"Well, at least you aren't both his wives," said the matron. "Don't think I never seen that. You might as well sit. It will be a while."

When Betty turned back to the room, she could not imagine who else could be waiting to see her father. The tarty-looking thing in the tight skirt and fake fur? The masculine one who could have been a matron herself? The redhead? Impossible.

She went to one of the long wooden benches, sat down, and arranged the ruffles of her Sunday skirt. The wood was filigreed with names and initials and dates. She ran her fingers over them and wondered why anyone would want to leave her name in such an awful place.

"So you are Karl's daughter," said a voice behind her. It startled her, and when she turned, she saw the woman with red hair. "I'm Luella Grundy."

When she put out her hand, Betty felt drawn to take it.

"My name is Betty," she said.

"I don't suppose Karl has ever spoken of me," Luella said.

She had a friendly face, though with a hint of hardness deep at the level of bone.

"What do they do when someone has two visitors?" asked Betty, because it was the least of her confusion.

"I imagine they go with a preference for blood," said Luella. "After maleness and wealth, that's the usual." She must have seen something come into Betty's face, because she immediately softened. "Don't worry," she said. "I was a secretary in his uncle's firm in Chicago when your father came in out of the North Woods smelling like a chimney."

"He took my mom and me to the North Woods once," said Betty.

"I helped him find his way in the city," said Luella. "He was really very sweet. But you know that, don't you? Then your mother arrived on the scene."

Betty looked to the concrete floor.

"Oh, my," said Luella. "I've given you the wrong idea. I was glad that he found your mother. He needed someone who could love the life I knew he was going to choose."

Again she read Betty's mind.

"The life of a farm town," said Luella. "The good bourgeois burgher's wife. Pillars of the community. I'm afraid I'm made differently. Tell your mother you met a crazy socialist who was trying to be a friend of the oppressed."

Betty moved down the wooden bench to give Luella a place to sit beside her.

"Of all the capitalists in the world, they came down on your father," said Luella. "My Joe says he must be a good man if they sent him to prison."

"Joe is your husband?" said Betty.

"Bourgeois marriage is hypocrisy," said Luella. "That's Marx and Engels."

"I'm not familiar with them," said Betty.

"Not surprising," Luella smiled, "in a banker's daughter."

She ran her fingers through her thick hair and then shook it out.

"What does Joe do for a living?" Betty asked.

"He operates a movie projector," said Luella.

"Marx Brothers," said Betty.

A tiny laugh escaped Luella.

"When I met Joe he was working at the Oriental Theater on Randolph Street," she said. "He could get me in free to pretty nearly any show in the Loop, he had so many friends. Then came the trouble, and he didn't have any friends anymore. When he got laid off, he found a job in a picture show in Lockport. It was pretty easy for me to get work there. Letting me learn bookkeeping was the one good thing your dad's uncle ever did for me. That and introducing me you to your dad. Do they have a movie theater in your little town?"

"Abbeville," said Betty.

"Abbeville," said Luella. "How is Abbeville dealing with all of this?"

"Some people better than others," said Betty.

"Smoke?" said Luella, holding out a pack of cigarettes and making a few of them pop up with a flip of the wrist.

"Oh my, no," said Betty. She had never seen a woman smoking before except on the big screen in Kankakee.

Luella took out a cigarette, tapped it on the bench, then pulled out a book of matches and struck one. The sulfur stung Betty's nose.

Luella leaned back on the bench and let the smoke roll in her mouth before gulping it down. She talked about what it had been like to be young in Chicago at the turn of the century, the World's Columbian Exposition, the Board of Trade, and Uncle John.

"That one was all business," she said.

"They say he managed to keep some of his money," Betty said.

"He wasn't a captain who'd go down with the ship," said Luella.

"My dad's brother kept his head above water, too," said Betty, "by pushing Dad under."

"The world is full of them," said Luella. "Joe was the one who saw in the paper that they'd sent your dad here. We started coming regular, it was so close to Lockport and all. Joe almost always comes along, but today he couldn't. I wish you had a chance to meet him. Another time. Your poor dad's going to be here for quite a while."

Betty didn't like to think of it that way. Two years ago she had been a silly little girl. The sentence was that long.

"Luella Grundy," said a voice. "Betty Schumpeter."

They stood.

"Maybe I should wait 'til you're done," Betty said.

"Come on, girl," said the woman. "You had the gumption to get this far."

She wished she had been born with a lot bigger store of gumption because this world seemed to require it.

The corridor took a couple of turns before it opened out into a larger room where the men sat on one side of a wall of chicken wire and the women sat on the other. Betty looked up and down the line at the inmates, all of them in the same faded gray, with black numbers across their chests.

"There he is," said Luella.

He had lost at least twenty pounds, which made the clothes hang from him.

"With all the weight coming off, you just keep getting younger and younger," Luella said. "You look like you did when I met you."

"My heavens," said Karl, a smile lighting him. "What did I do to deserve this bounty? Come here, Betty. Let me look at you."

The women reached out their hands. He touched both of them and then withdrew from Luella.

"Luella and I met when I was just a lad," he said.

"We had a talk about it," Betty said. "Your ears must have been burning."

As he looked at her, his ears actually did redden.

"You weren't supposed to come," he told Betty.

She wanted to press herself up against the wire and hug him the way he used to hug her when she was hurt.

"How are you doing, Karl?" Luella asked.

"Not bad," he said. "Not bad."

Betty kept her fingertips in contact with his, which were cold and seemed to lack the strength to push back.

"Are they feeding you?" Betty said.

"Don't forget to tell your mother how much I miss her cooking," he said.

"What can we do to make this easier for you?" Betty said.

"Be of a quiet heart," her father said. "That's what you can do. Forgive."

"I can't listen to this," Luella snapped. "You've got to fight back."

It startled Betty, but not her father.

"That isn't my plan," he said.

"See, that's why we weren't made for each other," Luella said.

"Your mother knows all about Luella," Karl told Betty. "I suppose it doesn't hurt that you know, too. She was the first big-city girl I'd ever met, and I was infatuated. Then your mother came to Chicago, and Luella disappeared."

"Let's not talk about it," said Luella.

"I have wanted to since way back then," Karl said, "but you vanished from the face of the earth. And then later, well, somehow it just was never the right moment to apologize. I think now is the time and place for penitence, don't you?"

Luella response was subdued. Even her hair seemed darker.

"One day," she said, "I hid near your rooming house and followed you when you came out. It wasn't hard to keep you from seeing me. You were off somewhere."

Luella watched the spot where Betty's fingers were in contact with her father's. Her own fingers stroked her bare, freckled forearm below the white cotton ruffles of her blouse. Her voice was low.

"You met her in the park," she said, "and then you walked to the beach. You talked all the way. I knew then that you would marry."

Luella gathered up her purse and stood.

"It's time for me to go," she said. "Joe will be waiting. We plan to stop somewhere along the way to eat, someplace charming, like I've always imagined Abbeville to be."

Now, ALMOST SEVEN decades later, as my mother sat in her living room at the retirement home, it still brought tears as she told it: Luella obviously still loving him, seeing him on the other side of the wire mesh, his fingers weakly touching my mother's, the metal rubbed shiny under them by countless hands reaching for what they could not have.

19

WITH THE VERY MODEST ADJUSTMENTS the system in those days provided for good behavior, Karl's release came a few days before Thanksgiving. The guards led him to the storage room, where he changed back into his clothes, which had grown as baggy as a clown's. Then they handed him a paper bag with his pocketknife and other personal effects. Sheriff Hawk was waiting for him at the gate.

"What are you doing here, John?" Karl asked.

"I took you away from Abbeville," the sheriff said, "and now I aim to bring you back."

They did not talk on the drive. Karl had nothing to say.

When they reached the house, it seemed to have aged a decade. The paint had lost the last of its color. A large crack had developed in the massive concrete front steps, which were covered with green moss, as if no one had trodden upon them since he had left. The porch screens had holes that had not been patched against the bees and wasps. Wasn't there even enough money to buy a couple of square inches of mesh?

He entered the porch and let the door slap closed behind him. The front door was, as always, unlocked to the world. He pushed it open, thinking of the marvel of doors that swung freely, the terror of what some doors opened onto.

The smell of fresh corn boiling on the old cookstove overwhelmed him. He put the paper bag down on the wooden bureau. The mirror above it caught his image. He did not belong here anymore.

Cristina came into the doorway of the kitchen and froze.

"We didn't expect you so soon," she said.

"They knocked a little time off," he said. "I should have found a way to let you know. Maybe Fred Krull can take me in."

He took a step back toward the door.

"Where do you think you're going?" Cristina said.

"I don't blame you not wanting me," he said.

She stepped forward and put her arms around him. At first he stood motionless. Then her embrace reached into him, and he held to her.

During his first days home he missed the prison rituals that had emptied time of meaning and made it light enough to bear. Now there was nothing to give it shape. It wasn't possible to revive his older habits: the early-morning visit to the grain elevator, the opening of the bank. The evening pinochle games were still going, but Karl could only bring himself to stand on the porch in the chill and look across the prairie grass and tracks toward the lights in the garage.

"They would welcome you," said Cristina.

"Because they pity me," he said.

Everywhere houses were slumping in disrepair. The paint of the elevator had faded to a dirty gray, and the words "Schumpeter Bros." in big black letters along its side were an accusation. Someone had nailed three boards across the Coliseum's door, and planking covered the windows. The only part of the building that still functioned was the tavern in the cellar.

Thanksgiving morning found Karl awake before dawn. There had been a stirring in him that had not permitted him to fall asleep even after Cristina had unaccountably given herself to him. Eventually he had drifted off, but only for a few hours. Then the stirring came again. He got dressed quietly in the bathroom and went out back for a pipe among the chickens. As he sat on a stump, the rooster came out of the coop, hopped up on an egg box, and preened. Then it reared back and crowed. Once. Twice. Three times.

"You made your point," Karl said.

The rooster crowed twice more.

"At least you know what you're good for," Karl said.

Suddenly an idea came into his head. Ideas were what got him in trouble. He shook it off, got up, and went to the basement, where he stoked the furnace until it was so fully ablaze that he had to close the cast-iron door with a poker. Then he climbed back up the stairs and went to work on the banked embers in the cookstove.

Soon Cristina was up and about. Then Betty arrived home. She was seventeen now and had finished high school early to take a job as a clerk in Potawatomi, earning room and board by continuing to keep house for the family she had worked for while she was in school. Karl hugged her and listened uncomfortably as she told him how much she had been able to pay off on the house.

"It's time to pick out our meal," he said to change the subject, then led the way to the chicken pen. Cristina chose a bird, and he wrung its neck.

"It will have to pass for turkey, I'm afraid," she said.

"I've always been partial to the smaller fowl," said Karl.

When it came to preparing the meal, Cristina was the impresario, a role Karl loved watching her play. It obviously annoyed their newly independent daughter, however, who with Karl was relegated to fetch-

ing and washing and peeling, sweeping and dusting and setting pictures aright on the walls. Soon Cristina had fresh bread in the oven. A
pie waited its turn, the bird sat trimmed up in a roasting pan, the veg-
etables in pots ready to be boiled.

"There's a service at the church this morning," Cristina said.

"I can't face them," Karl said. "You go. I'm sorry."

But she continued her preparations, and he went to the screen
porch and sat on the swing. The church bell pealed. Eventually he
heard the muffled sound of the choir and then the congregation singing the doxology. *Forever and ever. Amen.*

Eventually Cristina came to the door with a bowl of mashed potatoes and called him inside. Next she brought to the table green beans
she had put by from her garden and, of course, corn on the cob. There
were no cranberries, but there was plenty of stuffing, though little of it
had ever seen the inside of the bird. Finally she brought out the
chicken itself. It made the platter seem enormous.

"You first, Dad," said Betty.

Karl took a bit of white and brown meat, then passed the tray to his
daughter.

"Sit down, Mom," Betty said—a little sharply, Karl thought.

It must have been hard on both of them, with Betty paying for the
house and Cristina trying to hold on to her place in it.

Eventually the cook conceded that everything was in good enough
order that she could relax a moment before starting to fuss over the
pie. As she sat down, a knock came at the door. Cristina cast a nervous
look at Betty, who got up and opened it.

"He's here, isn't he?"

Karl recognized Henry Mueller's rough old voice.

"Of course he is," said Betty.

Eyes upon tablecloth, Karl heard the rustle of people entering.

Then he snapped to his feet as if it were an inspection. He did not know what to do among decent people anymore.

Before him stood Rose Stroeger and the Tragues, Henry Mueller, Fred Krull, Robert Hesse and his wife, even George Loeb. One bore a bowl of sweet potatoes, the next a tray of cranberries, then sweet corn, mince and pumpkin pies, and finally a large and proper bird.

Finally Rose stepped up to him and gave him a hug that loosened everyone's tongue. At some point Hesse, who had bought the Schumpeter Bros.' implement inventory, asked Karl to come to work for him. "There's nobody the farmer of Cobb County respects more than you."

"It's mighty kind of you, Robert," said Karl. "But I don't have a taste for the business anymore."

"You've got to do something," said Mueller. "There are only so many bees you can swat."

Karl looked over at the table laden with their offerings. In the middle was the scrawny, picked-over chicken. He pointed at it.

"I'm going to sell those," he said.

This was the idea the rooster had brought him.

"Sell what?" said Hesse.

"People still have enough money to buy a chicken," he said.

"There's time for you to think about it," said Hesse.

"I got to grant you this," said Mueller. "A lot more folks will be in the market for a bird than for one of those big International Harvesters in Robert's lot."

"It'll come back," said Hesse.

Cristina pulled a chair in from the kitchen and squeezed it between the others at the table.

"Won't you sit down and join us?" she said.

"We'll all be together tomorrow in the church basement with the leftovers—like always," said Rose. "Today you need to be a family."

The others took her hint and began to leave until finally only old Henry was left.

"I held open the job tending the schoolhouse," he said. "It ain't buying and selling chickens. And it don't pay much. But it's steady."

All this talk of positions made Karl wary. When you had learned to give everything up, you had to be careful about taking anything back again.

"Thank you very kindly, Henry," said Karl. "I would've mown that raggedy lawn anyway just because I have to look at it. But I'll give your idea careful consideration."

"You do that, Karl," Mueller said.

20

KARL TOOK THE JOB AT THE SCHOOLHOUSE and submerged himself in it. From dawn until the children arrived and again after they left, he washed and polished and swept and scrubbed, from bell tower to basement. Anything human hands could accomplish without money, he did. Then each morning before the students showed up, he disappeared back into his house.

"Why don't you at least stick around and see their faces?" asked the cute young teacher who handled the lower grades.

"Little ones shouldn't be around convicted felons," said Karl.

"Oh, pshaw, Mr. Schumpeter," she said. "Seems to me everybody in this town knows you better than you do."

When the children were all safely inside, Karl would come back out of his house and work on the school grounds in the cold. The swing set got new seats cut from Fritz's scrap pile. Rusted swivels shone in the winter sun. Come the first thaw, he would work the ground for landscaping—beds for wildflowers, holes for some nice trees transplanted from the woods at Otter Creek. From time to time he would see a small face in the corner window where the teacher sent boys who were acting up, their faces all mischief and contrition. Karl always turned away.

With the spring the balance of his time shifted almost entirely to the grounds. Digging, raking, planting, weeding, mowing.

"Do you think you're Frederick Law Olmsted?" asked Henry Mueller.

"There's no reason these children don't deserve something as nice in its way as the park he made for the Exposition," he said.

As the school year drew to a close, he came to the end of the large tasks he could do without resources. He knew that during the summer he would not even be able to busy himself cleaning up inside each afternoon, and there was only so much grass to mow, so many weeds to pull. So he went to Henry and suggested a reduction in the monthly amount he was paid.

"I have a better idea," Henry said.

"I'm not one for charity," said Karl.

"You know I'm not one for giving it," said Henry. "What would it take to bring that old schoolhouse up to the level of the best in the county?"

"I haven't been to the other schools in the county."

"Up to your standards, then," said Henry.

They were seated in Mueller's parlor, which was much smaller than Karl's. This made Karl feel awkward, as if they should trade places now that Henry was the power in Abbeville. Not that Henry would go for it. He was a smart man. He wanted to live small.

"I'd have to work it out," Karl said. "It would take some capital investment, though. Not so much. The boiler's good. The pipes are sound. The roof's okay, though it could probably use a layer of shingles. Better still, I could tear off the old first. They're two deep already."

"You write it all down," said Henry.

"I'll do that. Thank you."

"And be sure to include the hours it will take of your labor."

"No extra charge there," said Karl. "I'd just stay occupied, the way I have been."

"The town's been getting a free ride off you, Karl. I want you paid for *all* the work you do."

"I still owe the town a debt," said Karl.

"Everybody owed everybody. That was the mess of it. But if anybody paid, you did. Now the slate's clean, and we pay as we go. You count your hours into the plan."

"Henry . . ." Karl said.

"Count them," said Mueller.

No two-room schoolhouse ever had as beautiful a capital budget as Abbeville's got from Karl. He used some old ledger paper he found in a drawer at the bank and wrote it all out in his careful hand. Mueller barely looked at it before giving the nod, but Karl did not care. He would account for every cent he spent with the same attention to detail he had invested in the plan, because precision was a kind of atonement.

"By the way, Karl," Henry said, "Maude has decided it's time to retire as postmistress."

"That's too bad," said Karl. "She's still got some tread on her."

"Wants to kick back and sit on the porch watching the world go by," said Henry.

"Well, she better have a lot of tread on her, then," said Karl, "because it is going to be a while before much of the world passes through Abbeville."

"I want you to take her place," said Mueller.

"I'm going to be pretty busy."

"Hellfire, man," said Henry, "you can't turn down the government."

Karl looked at his hands.

"They got rules against it," he said.

"It's Congressman Pease's appointment, and he got everything waived already. So I ain't asking you to break any law."

"Pease is mighty young," said Karl. "What does he know about me?"

"What his constituents tell him," said Henry. "If they could waive the rules against it, you could probably give him a run in the next primary."

"Henry."

Mueller looped his arm over Karl's shoulder, as if he might be the one planning to give young Pease a run.

"Trust me on this," he said.

"Isn't you I don't trust," said Karl.

"My nephew isn't going to give you any more trouble, Karl. That's all over. He's got plenty of his own troubles to attend to, the way I hear it."

Karl was silent.

"Then it's done," said Mueller. "Maude will break you in on Friday. Monday it's all yours."

"I don't know what to say," said Karl.

"Let me help. 'What does it pay?' That's what you should say, because sweet as Betty is, you got to start having your own. That's one determined daughter you've got there."

"She likes to be a mother hen, all right," Karl said.

"I wonder where she gets that," said Henry.

As KARL PURGED HIMSELF through sweat, Fritz seemed to prosper. The talk of Abbeville was that when Karl went down and Ansel looked the other way with Fritz, it had strengthened Fritz's standing with his politician friends, who had been holding their breath since Ansel began frisking Fritz's business. Nobody knew that Fritz was bulletproof only because of Karl's plea bargain. It looked to the world like he had enough influence to make even the county prosecutor back away. Fritz was a man to deal with, all right. So when there was money for roads again, he got more than his share. Little as this was, it still drove Betty to fury.

The first time the two brothers talked had been in January. Betty had come home that Friday for the weekend. The weather was cold enough that Karl had fired up the furnace to supplement the heat thrown off by the cookstove. A little snow had fallen. Not enough to shovel, but it had stuck on the trees and lawn.

Karl was in his rocker. The radio was tuned, for Betty's benefit, to a station playing swing music from the College Inn in Chicago. Karl was working on the mushy end of a cold cigar when a car came around the corner, its headlights flashing across the windows. Betty and Cristina came out of the kitchen.

"It's him," said Betty.

Karl waited a moment and then stood. Betty went to the window.

"He isn't even getting out," she said. "Look at him, just sitting there as smug as can be."

"He probably knows that if he comes into this house with you here," Karl said, "he risks leaving without his skin."

"Don't let him make you go to him, Dad," Betty said. "Don't you do it."

"Betty," said Cristina.

Karl went to the front door and pulled on his jacket. As he reached for the knob, Betty started toward him. Cristina stepped in between them.

"Don't say another word against him," Cristina whispered. "He's your father's brother. That's what he is."

The two brothers did not talk for long. Karl did not even enter the car. When Fritz pulled away, Karl stood in the road for a time, then trudged back to the house.

"What did he want?" Betty demanded.

"Betty," warned Cristina.

"I'm just asking," said Betty.

Karl walked past her and went to his rocker.

"He asked me if I needed money," he said.

Cristina's hand on Betty's shoulder tightened.

"I told him that we'd get along just fine," Karl said.

"Good for you, Karl," said Cristina.

"He's having a hard time with this," Karl said.

"He is!" said Betty, despite her mother's grip.

"By the look of it, he's got money coming in, but a lot more going out," said Karl. "It's got to be weighing on him."

"There's weight all around," said Cristina.

21

ON ROBERT HESSE'S IMPLEMENT LOT stood a rusted old Ford truck with rotting wood plank sides. Its passenger window would not roll up, so the seats were faded beyond color and sharp with mildew. Its engine had not started for years. Two of its wheels were missing, and it leaned to the left, where its axles rested on large cement blocks.

"How much do you want for it?" Karl asked Hesse.

"It ain't even good for parts anymore," said Hess.

"If I can get it working," said Karl, "I'll pay you a fair price."

"I ought to pay you for taking a piece of rubbish off my property," said Hesse.

These days things generally just stayed where they died, cars stripped down by the side of the road, half-tumbled-in chicken coops, barns without roofs. In some places whole building projects stood abandoned. You could see just where the money had stopped—the moment preserved, like Pompeii under the ash.

"I will pay," said Karl.

Next he went to Fritz and asked if he could use his mechanics' tools.

"I'll have one of my crew fix the truck up for you," Fritz said, so distracted he seemed barely present, as if fixing a vehicle were too small a problem for either of them to trifle with.

"I guess I'd rather do it myself," said Karl.

"What do you know about automobiles?"

"Where I've been, you learn them right down to the license plates," said Karl.

Fritz froze like a rabbit sensing the shadow of an eagle. Then, whatever the predator was, it passed, and he looked at his wristwatch.

"Are you all right?" Karl asked.

"I'll have one of my boys go to the implement lot and tow it on over to the garage," said Fritz.

"Don't bother," said Karl. "Honest effort is what I need right now."

"You sound like that crazy socialist lady who used to visit you in prison," said Fritz.

"Who told you that?"

"Harley tells everybody she was quite a looker," said Fritz.

A few days later in the chill of a clear spring dawn, Karl went to the lot, mounted on the truck's axles two bald tires he had scrounged, wrenched the gearshift into neutral, and, with one hand on the steering wheel, began rocking it with his shoulder. Whatever lubrication the moving parts might once have known had long since fossilized.

The trick was to keep the front wheels straight, which was no small matter on the bumpy ground. Every time the wheels turned a little to the left or right, he lost momentum and had to redouble his efforts. Still, eventually the truck reached the road.

Just as it did, he felt something in his lower belly give way. He struggled to catch his breath, a tide of nausea coming over him along with the terrible thought that he might fail at even this simple task.

"What in the hell are you trying to do?" said Fred Krull, who had come up from the elevator.

"Taking some exercise," Karl managed to get out.

"Why not just go to the pasture and lift a cow?"

"I've got to get this machine to Fritz's garage where I can fix it up," said Karl.

"You think you're going to be able to push that thing a mile all by yourself?"

"It'll make the repairs seem easy," Karl said.

"I have half a mind just to sit down on my porch over there and watch your ornery soul try to get this junk up the crossing grade," said Krull.

The pain had begun to draw together and localize in Karl's groin. He put his fingers tentatively on the tender spot and felt a bulge.

Meanwhile, Krull enlisted the two Wills—Trague and Hoenig— along with George Loeb into the effort.

"My garage ain't good enough for you?" Trague said.

"I'm not going to start taking handouts," said Karl.

"Well, it sure ain't that with Fritz," said Hoenig, "with all he owes you."

"Nobody owes anybody anything," said Karl. "It all got washed out, like deadfall in a flood."

They arrayed themselves around the truck and got it rolling again. Karl steered as they pushed, and even that took his breath away.

When they reached the shed, hot and sweating, Fritz's roadster was in back. All you could see of it was the grill and fancy hood ornament poking past the far wall. Karl figured Fritz must have left it for one of his boys to tune up.

"I'm sure there's water around here somewhere," said Karl as the truck rolled to a stop in front of the closed plank doors of the shed.

"I got to be running along," said Krull.

"Store needs opening," said Hoenig.

"Garage, too," said Trague.

"I wouldn't mind getting my wind," said Loeb. "I'll just sit here in the truck for a while."

Karl opened the side door of the shed. Inside it was dark. He felt his way to the big front doors and unbolted them. Their bottoms scraped the dry, dead earth.

As the sun streamed in, it revealed benches covered with tools and rags, a foot-pedaled grinding machine, barrels of lubricant, tubs of grease. Belts, gears, and gaskets hung from the walls. The working area of the floor was black with spent oil, which gave the place its odor.

Karl sensed a presence.

"Fritz?" he called.

Loeb was sprawled out in the cab of the truck as if he were fixing to sleep. The other three had started toward the road. Karl went to the workbench and put his foot to the pedal to spin the grinding wheel. He picked up various wrenches and mallets, weighing each in his hand. The heavier ones communicated directly to his groin. He held each of them aloft, testing the pain, learning it.

When he went back to the truck, Loeb was snoring. Karl quietly opened the driver's-side door and put his shoulder to it. The pain was solid now, a prison wall. He would not be able to get the vehicle into the shed by himself.

He closed the door.

"Fritz?" he said again. Loeb stirred but did not awaken.

Silence.

Karl lifted the hood of the truck carefully. Karl had known little of engines until Stateville. Some enlightened soul at the prison had decided that fixing automobiles would one day be in enough demand that an employer might overlook a good mechanic's bad record. So prison employees brought their cars into the shop behind the walls—

ABBEVILLE

the sedan of the warden, the flivvers of the guards. Karl liked working on the engines the best. Gasoline and air in, energy and waste out: metabolism. While others went to the law books in the library to fashion hopeless appeals, he immersed himself in oil and grease, making something live that had been dead. Summer to winter. Winter to spring.

Under the hood of the truck in the bright sunlight outside Fritz's shed, he pushed on the hoses, which were brittle, tried to spin the fan, and checked the radiator, which was so rusted he could see the ground through it. He screwed the cap back on, then went around to the back of the garage.

The sun was behind Fritz's car, so all Karl could see at first was its silhouette. As he drew closer and the angle of the light changed, he noticed that the windows were spotted. It wasn't like Fritz to leave mud on his car.

Karl took two more steps.

"Oh, Fritz," he said.

When he opened the door, his brother's head and shoulders dropped over the edge of the seat. A little blood from the wound in his skull dripped to the dry earth, which absorbed it readily. In the shadow of the running board lay Fritz's revolver. Karl leaned over and picked it up. He held it in his hand a moment, feeling how small it was against what it had wrought upon the poor, terrified rabbit. Then he put the pistol in his waistband and went to tell the others.

197

22

HENRY MUELLER HAD BEEN WRONG about Harley Ansel. At the coroner's inquest Ansel argued that the cause of Fritz's death was homicide. First he questioned George Loeb, who testified that he had been sleeping in the cab of the truck when he'd heard Karl cry out. When he went behind the shed with Karl a few minutes later, he testified, he found Fritz "stone-cold dead."

"Was Karl holding anything?" Ansel asked.

"No."

"Let me try again. Did you see a weapon?" said Ansel.

"Karl had picked up Fritz's pistol," said Loeb.

"How did you know it was Fritz's?" Ansel asked.

"Whose else would it have been?" said Loeb. "Harley, you know whose it was."

Ansel turned his back on the witness for a moment and consulted a sheet of paper.

"Did you have a watch?" Ansel asked.

"In my pocket."

"Did you check it?"

"No, sir," said Loeb.

"Then you cannot be sure how long you slept," said Ansel.

"I couldn't have slept through a gunshot," said Loeb.

"That's not what your wife says," said Ansel.

For once in his life George Loeb stood his ground.

"You keep my wife out of it," he said.

Will Trague, Fred Krull, and Will Hoenig all testified that they were a couple of hundred yards down the road from the shed when they heard a cry, then a minute later saw Karl coming from behind it.

"We went back to see what was the matter," Krull testified. "That body was cold. It had been dead for quite a while."

"Are you a doctor?" asked Ansel.

"No, but I've seen my share of dead people," Krull said.

"So yours is a layman's opinion," said Ansel.

"Even a horse don't go stiff the minute you put her down," said Krull.

Finally Ansel called Karl to testify.

"You don't have to, you know," said the coroner. "It's your right."

"I'm not afraid to face this man," said Karl.

"You're a lot better at looking out for other people than looking out for yourself," said the coroner. "I'll let you testify, but I'm going to do the questioning, if that's all right with you."

"This is highly irregular," Ansel protested.

"It isn't a court of law, Harley," said the coroner. "Now Karl, I've got one question only. Did you shoot your brother?"

"I did not," said Karl. "I . . ."

"One question, one answer," said the coroner. "Go back and be seated."

In his closing statement Ansel theorized that Karl had gone to the garage earlier, killed Fritz, then returned to get the truck and arrange his alibi.

"He had the motive," Ansel argued. "He went to jail and Fritz went free."

"Who made that happen, Harley?" shouted old Henry Mueller from the back of the crowd.

"Now, no more of that, Henry," said the coroner. "I've heard enough. The death was a suicide, plain and simple. Everybody knows Fritz was living way beyond what he could afford. And this time he didn't have his brother there to catch him when he started to fall. I'm sorry about your loss, Karl. You must have loved your brother terribly to have done for him the way you did."

AFTER THE INQUEST Karl threw himself back into fixing up the schoolhouse. He started with the ceilings, and right away his neck cricked up. That night he squirmed on the pillow searching for a comfortable position. Cristina heard his restlessness and came in with the liniment.

"You could slow down, you know," she said, massaging it into his muscles.

"That feels good, Mama," he said.

"Would you like something that feels better?" she asked.

"What's got into you?"

"I guess it's the liniment," she said.

"I'm going to have to get sore more often," Karl said.

One day a few months later John Hawk arrived at their door unannounced. Cristina saw him and let out a cry. Betty came running from the kitchen. Karl woke from a catnap in his rocker and looked out the window.

"It's all right," he said, rising.

He opened the front door as Hawk was coming up the steps.

"Come on in, John," he said.

Hawk stayed just inside the doorway, removing his hat and bowing to the ladies.

"What does Harley Ansel want from us now?" said Betty.

"He's dead," said Hawk. "Ran a hose from the exhaust into the passenger compartment. I figured you'd want to know."

"Why?" said Cristina.

"There were debts," said Hawk.

"Well, at least he found out how it feels," said Betty.

"Then there were padded invoices to the county and state, fines collected but never delivered to the treasurer. And, of course, the lady."

"Lady?" Betty perked up.

"A lot of people knew," said Hawk. "Seemed like everybody did except Louise. There'll be a paternity suit, I suppose, though I don't know why. There's nothing left to fight over."

"Poor Louise," said Cristina.

Karl, too, felt for Harley's wife. Felt for everyone.

Forever after, Betty saw Ansel's suicide as a myth of guilt hounding a man to his punishment. The town chattered for a time about whether Fritz and Ansel had been in cahoots somehow, about how Ansel's accusation of Karl at the inquest could have been to cover his own crime.

But Karl knew that Ansel, like Fritz, had simply been crushed by history's downstroke, and everyone bore responsibility for it. The Depression was the sum of millions of individual flaws. History was as relentless as a force of nature, but in this case what man suffered, he made.

The sheer scale of it drove a person back to palpable things sized to his hands. Brushstrokes on a door frame. Liniment rubbed in where it hurt. For Karl small things became the world, a world he could feel at home in.

Soon he got the old truck running and began taking the vehicle on regular runs to Chicago. He had enlarged his own chicken yard to the limits of the lot. At first he took only his own birds and eggs to market, but soon he was also taking others' on consignment. Whenever he lifted a crate into the back of the truck, pain pushed against his truss.

Monday through Friday he rose before dawn and took a constitutional up to the cemetery, where he sat with his back to the same tree and watched which part of which stone the sun rose over, solstice to equinox to solstice again. It gave him comfort to know the two days of the year it would eventually rise directly over his.

After opening up the school and tending the chickens, he met the southbound 8:07 as it threw off its leather mail sack, which bounced and rolled until it came to rest near his feet. He put it into his cart and took it to the old bank building, which had been bought for next to nothing at auction by the federal government to serve as a post office. Next he drove to farms around Abbeville picking up chickens and eggs, then returned to sort the letters and occasional packages, usually finishing before noon. He had lunch with Cristina, tended the birds, and delivered the mail by cart to the homes in town, gathering outbound letters as he went. These he put back into the leather sack, which he carried in the cart to the big cast-iron pole. He hung the sack on the armature just in time to be snatched up by the northbound 3:47. By then class was out at the school, and the building was ready for cleaning.

Weekends had a different rhythm. He still rose before dawn. Cristina still made him breakfast. But instead of doing chores, he left for Chicago, loading the eggs and fowl in the morning and returning empty the following evening. In good weather he slept in the truck. When it got cold he stayed in a run-down hotel near the farmer's market. If the weather was inclement he wore a great sea-green slicker and black rubber hat like somebody from *Captains Courageous*, which sat on his bookshelf alongside the Zane Greys.

Then war came again. This time there were no effigies. Even before the call went out, French and Germans went to the infantry, to the armored cavalry, to the B24s over Europe and Japan. The demand for everything, including chickens and eggs, began to rise. Eventually the farms had to feed not only the Army but all of Europe.

Abbeville prospered, this time without Karl's guidance. The chicken business did not require him to drive all the way to Chicago anymore. The government had a supply point in Kankakee that paid top dollar, which meant he could take care of everything on Saturday and on Sunday go to church with Cristina again and sing with conviction in his booming monotone. *Forever and ever. Amen.*

Karl was glad for Abbeville, glad to be steadily at Cristina's side, glad that Betty had met Brendan Bailey while she was up in Chicago working in an office. One weekend she brought him home on the C&EI in his Army uniform. Karl took an immediate liking to him. He was an Irishman with perhaps a little too much of the blarney, but he seemed steady on his feet.

When he went off on maneuvers, Betty moved back home and worked at the school across the street, having earned her teaching certificate in Chicago. Every morning Karl laid a fire for her in the school's two potbelly stoves and opened windows a crack to allow a draft.

Then, a week after Pearl Harbor, Brendan left for California bound for the South Pacific. Betty took a civilian train and followed him. She stayed the whole Christmas break in San Francisco while he waited in the Cow Palace with thousands of others. Cristina worried when Betty returned without a ring.

Then a ring came in the mail. Heaven only knew where Brendan had gotten it or with what. It was small, but to Betty it was the Hope diamond. And she needed all the hope she could muster when she learned that he had shipped out from Hawaii to places the censors did not even let him name. Eventually he reached Okinawa. Then Truman dropped the bomb, and he came home.

They held the wedding in the Evangelical and Reformed Church, catered by the ladies of the town, who would not let Cristina make so much as a pie. It was the only time Karl had ever seen her lose control of a kitchen.

Brendan found a job in radio. Soon he started substituting on the farm report—on the strength, he said, of his agricultural cultivation. When he and Betty came to visit, the town met the train as if they were celebrities.

He was as outgoing as Betty was reserved, with a beefy, smoky laugh, which came from him often, especially after a taste or two of the schnapps.

Karl sensed something dark behind it. One day as they walked along Otter Creek, he decided to ask.

"You still think about it?"

"What's that, sir?" said Brendan, addressing Karl as if he were an officer.

"What you saw and did," said Karl.

"It's over now," said Brendan.

"I still think about Verdun," said Karl.

"That was a bad one," said Brendan.

They kept walking, and Karl did not know whether he had crossed a line he should not have. They reached the shack and sat down on the open porch.

"If you ever want to talk," Karl said.

"This is a real peaceful spot," said Brendan.

23

OVER THE YEARS MY FATHER AND GRAND-
father spent a lot of time together at Otter
Creek. When I was old enough, they started to bring me with them.
It was not very exciting watching them sit there looking down at the
crick.

"You ever dip a line?" asked my father.

"Nothing in there but catfish and moccasin," Grampa said.

I wandered down the high bank, hoping to see a poisonous snake.
The water smelled as if something terrible lay rotting on the bottom. When I climbed back up, I saw that I had gone about a hundred yards downstream from the shack. The two men had their backs
to me, smoke rising in puffs in the windless air. I crept up behind
them.

"Has Betty cleared her plans for us with you?" Grampa asked.

"I grew up with seven brothers and sisters. Then there was the bar-
racks. We'll get along fine."

My father pulled out his pack of Camels, tapped one out, and lit it.

"What does Mrs. Schumpeter think?" he asked.

"She knows it is going to be Betty's house," said Grampa, "Betty's kitchen."

My father stood up.

"It must have been hard on her," he said, "having her daughter take over things."

"It was hard on Betty, too," Grampa said. "She never had a chance to be young."

My father lit a cigarette and flicked a fly away from his face.

"You've done damned well all on your own so far," he said.

"Wouldn't even have a house if it wasn't for Betty," said Grampa.

"Is that the reason? That you owe her?" my father said.

"One of them," said Grampa. "She worries about us so."

"When you think on it," said my father, "don't think about Betty or me or the boy. Do what's right for the two of you for once. No-body else."

As I heard them talking, I didn't really appreciate what Grandma and Grampa moving in with us might mean to me. Mostly I guess I liked the idea of not having to leave my friends to go to Abbeville in order to be around Grampa.

He and my father sat in silence long enough that I thought about going back down to Otter Creek to see if any snakes had shown up. I may even have started backing away from them when Grampa started to speak in that tone of his that seemed to have a smile in it.

"Before we do anything, there's something I've been thinking about for a long while," he said.

"What's that?" my father said.

"It's time for George to make the acquaintance of a proper river," Grampa said. "And I know just the one."

. . .

IN THE CRAMPED CAR seat on the long trip north Karl felt every minute of his age. Brendan did the driving; Karl was relegated to reading the map. George sat in the back seat with his comics.

When they reached the river, Karl revived. He helped Brendan pull the canoe off the roof of the car and drag it to the water. Then he taught son-in-law and grandson the rudiments of paddling.

Once under way, they glided past snaggy, fallen timber, over gravel riffles that scraped the bottom of the canoe, and into the flat, dark water of sand holes that big brown trout sounded upon the appearance of the sun. Karl had seated himself at the rear of the canoe so he could handle the steering.

"This is a good spot to get started," he said, turning the oar until the current pushed back against it with a familiar thrum. They drifted toward a low, sandy bank where a little high grass might grab your fly but would always give it back.

Karl had to take Brendan's hand to be able to get out of the canoe. The trouble with age was that you thought about everything too much. You thought about the rocking canoe. You thought about whether you could time your movement to it. You thought about cracking your hip or banging your head. Karl took a step, and his right foot landed in sand on the shallow side. It was awkward to get the left foot over the gunwale, but Brendan helped, and there he was, immersed in his element again.

Betty had thought the whole expedition was crazy.

"I want you to bring him home whole, Brendan," she had said, "not in a box."

"Or if it is a box," said Karl, "at least one also packed with ice and decent trout."

He stayed close to the bank, pulling his waders out of the sucking sand with every step. In the canoe he had rigged up the rod with an elk-hair caddis, which was fairly easy to see on the water. His fingers had trembled a bit, but the eye of the hook was mercifully large. Now, as he flipped a backcast, the timing came right back to him. Even a man in his eighties could cast a fly because the power was in knowing how to use the flex of the rod, not the withered muscles of the arm.

He showed Brendan and George the motion: Accelerate and stop. Accelerate and stop. Ten o'clock and 2 o'clock.

"Now you try," he said.

Brendan was not a natural athlete, but he controlled the line and kept his casts short and manageable, never overextending himself, never getting into trouble. Betty had married well.

"Now George," said Karl.

"It's okay," said the boy.

"Aw, give it a go," said Karl. "Hear that gurgling? That's the sound of a fish calling your name."

George took the rod and attempted a cast, but after the line died in a messy clump in front of him a few times, he was ready to give up.

Karl took his grandson's arm to lead him through the stroke. George perked up when he felt Karl's old hands upon him. On one cast, a little rainbow trout actually took the fly in the riffles.

"Good work," Karl said as George reeled it in. "Now you are a man."

Karl popped the hook from the fish's mouth and let the trout dart away. It was not too long before they got another. Brendan had the luck this time. But it really did not require much. The river was bountiful. Karl sidearmed a shot deep under an overhanging tree and hooked a big brown. He handed the rod to Brendan to land it.

When it was George's turn again, the boy put the fly into the grass and deadfall as often as he put it into the stream. Karl had Brendan retrieve it when he could, tied on a new caddis when he couldn't.

"I learned to fish from a fellow who said there are only two rules," said Karl, recalling Hoekstra's voice from long ago. "Rule number one:

You have to fish where the fish are. Rule number two: The fish are in the water."

As George and his father traded off the rod, Karl concentrated on the current, feeling connected with all Creation through the drift of the fly and the eyes of fish and fisherman fixed on it, below and above.

"If you cast just a little more slack," Karl advised Brendan, "I think you'll reach that fish before the fly starts to drag."

On the next cast George's father did what Karl had suggested, and a nice fish finished the lesson.

Karl could have stayed there until nightfall. He could have been content simply watching the water slide past in an endless sheet. But they weren't outfitted for camping overnight.

"We'd better go," he said. "It's a longer paddle than you'd think from the map."

"I just want to try that one spot over there," said Brendan. "I've been saving it till the end. Come on, George. Let's see if we've learned anything."

They moved downriver around the bend until Karl could no longer see them. He stood in the current, thinking about all that had been swept away and all that had drifted to him unearned. He took several steps until the force of the water was about as much as he dared.

When he was younger, he had liked to wade in after dark, lusting for the big fish that only then came out to feed. In truth he was also attracted by the black pull of the current. It had been at this place, surrounded by the wasteland left by logging, that he had first felt the darkness at the center of things. He had felt it again in France. Then in prison. Then with Fritz. Now it came to him once more as he stood up to his fragile old knees in the black, flowing water. He closed his eyes and felt a great, perpetual movement drawing him. He barely had strength to resist. Nor did he want to. Eyes closed, he knew this would be his last time in the river. But he did not feel the least sense of loss. He accepted darkness as part of the cycle of light, and he was ready. The recognition of this came to him mysteriously from the depths, like the grace of a fish to a well-presented fly.

24

ON THE DAY THAT WAS TO BE HIS LAST AS postman Grampa took me in tow and pushed the handcart up to every door, even when there wasn't any mail to put in the box. Everywhere there were handshakes, hugs, and farewells. But when we got to Henry Mueller's place, there was something more.

"Are you sure you really want this, Karl?" Mueller said.

"Betty's got to do what she thinks is best," Grampa said.

"With all due respect, it don't say on that deed to your house that she owns you and Cristina, too," said Mueller.

Grampa let the cart down on its stubby back legs.

"'Tisn't the house, Henry. 'Tisn't a piece of paper and whose name is on it. With Cristina slowing down so, well, at some point I know I won't be able to handle it anymore."

"Betty is awfully quick to take charge," said Mueller.

"It brought us through the bad times," Grampa said.

"What about Cristina?"

I leaned back against the cart, listening, though I thought maybe I shouldn't be.

"Deep down she knows Betty's right," Grampa said.

"She stuck with you, Karl, didn't she?" said Mueller. "She loved you richer and poorer."

"Funny," Grampa said, "turned out easier poorer."

"Well, I haven't filled your jobs yet, just in case," said Mueller. "Because poorer ain't so great."

When we finished the rounds, we returned the cart to its place under the eaves of the old bank, put the outgoing mail we had collected into the empty leather sack, and dragged it inside until the late-afternoon train.

"What's in that old safe back there?" I asked.

"Dead mice and ideas," Grampa said.

"Can I see?"

"The ideas are invisible," Grampa said, "like ghosts. You want to lock them up tight so they don't haunt you."

We left the bank building and walked past the grain elevator toward the tracks. Along the way we had to step over a concrete foundation overgrown with weeds. I had used it a hundred times to set cans on for pinging with my rifle.

"What was here before?" I asked.

"Power," Grampa said and kept on walking.

"Once I thought I'd build a fort on it to conquer the Indians," I said.

"And I thought I was going to conquer the night," Grampa said. "Let's pick up the pace a little, George. Some of the work we've got to get done needs sunlight."

The schoolhouse stood so tall, perched atop a high cellar, that you might have expected four rooms rather than only two. To get the mower out Grampa had to hop it up a number of steps, which were well worn from years of this practice.

He had no intention of having me do any real work. He never did, which was one of the many things that endeared him to me. I sat on a stump and watched him push the old hand mower back and forth, back and forth, lapping by no more than an inch, lost to the world the way he had been on the river casting a fly.

"Got to remember to leave a note listing all the chores that have to be done here regular," he said when he finished.

He pulled the cellar door shut behind him, sliding the hasp of the bolt lock to.

"Got to put the key back in old Henry's hands," he said. "There's lots to think about still, George. Lots to do."

The schoolhouse was empty. Inside it smelled of lunches with milk. Grampa went to the closet and pulled out a big, long-brushed broom and an enormous tin dustpan. In the closet stood a barrel. He slid off the top, reached down, and came up with a Hills Bros. coffee can full of sawdust that had the aroma of oil and candle wax.

"You take command of the spreading and I'll do the pushing," said Grampa. "First, though, we've got to make ourselves a space."

Together we moved all the little desks and chairs in the north room to one side, leaving a broad, scuffed expanse of varnished pine.

"I need you to stay a little ahead of me," said Grampa. "Pretend you are sowing oats."

"I don't know how," I said.

"I'll show you."

Grampa laid down the sawdust in a quarter moon with a broad, sweeping motion of his right arm. The first time I tried, the sawdust landed in a clump.

"I thought we might need a bit more of it there, where the marks are the worst," I explained.

"Spreading it evenly straight through the swing will do just fine, George."

Once I got the hang of it, we needed just three passes to finish the part we had cleared of desks and chairs. The used cleaning compound lay in a neat line at the near end of the floor. I leaned over the dustpan as Grampa swept it in.

"You can throw it in the trash can over there," Grampa said. "We'll burn it later. The wax makes for a pretty flame."

When I looked back, the floor glowed in the setting sun.

"Now the other half," Grampa said. "This time we'll have to lift the desks and stay on our tiptoes so that we don't scrape a heel."

When we were finished with both rooms and the hall, the floors in every direction were as void of human imprint as a beach smoothed by waves. Grampa tilted his head to make sure that the job was right from every angle. Of course, in the morning the kids would obliterate our work. But for that moment when the children arrived, the school would shine.

I don't know whether or not he thought of it as the last time he would be able to look back on gainful labor. But the way he talked, he seemed content that others would follow—other caretakers, other postmen, other generations of the family, other rivers down to the end of time when the purpose of all would reveal itself, or would not.

We went out and put the trash and sawdust in the circle of blackened rocks at the back of the lawn. Grampa pulled out a kitchen match, struck it against the sole of his shoe, and tossed it on the pile, which whumped into flame. As it burned, we sat silently nearby, like ancient Indians raising prayers at a sacred spot on the endless plains.

WHEN EVERYONE ELSE had gone to bed, Karl and Cristina sat together in the kitchen.

"I guess we won't be warming milk on this cookstove many more times," said Karl.

"Well, you've got prices marked on everything we might warm it in," said Cristina.

"Did I go too high, do you think?" said Karl. "I don't want anybody to feel I'm gouging."

"Do you still have a bottle of schnapps?" asked Cristina.

She could still surprise him even after all the years.

"Why, I do believe there's some in the cellar," he said.

"No price tag on it for the sale?"

"Nope."

"How long have you had it down there for a secret nip?" she said.

"Every man needs something to hide," Karl said.

When he brought it up, it had a heavy coating of dust.

"See," he said. "Hardly touched."

"Blow it off outside, please," she said.

Karl went to the back steps and rubbed the glass down with his hands. Cristina took out two glasses that she had promised to a cousin. They were heavy crystal. She had bought them in Chicago just before their wedding. All six in the set had survived, largely because they had always been too good to use.

Karl poured, the bottle's neck tapping the lip of the glass like code. She let him pour a fair amount, more than he ever remembered her taking, and this emboldened him to give himself as much as he pleased.

"It's going to be a lot different," Cristina said.

Karl lifted his glass and said, "To the next fifty years."

Cristina lifted her glass, too, a little more slowly, and let it be touched.

"I'm not sure how many more years I have," she said.

"At Betty's," he said, "whatever happens, somebody will be there."

"I won't be cooking for you anymore," Cristina said.

"You deserve someone to do for you for a change," he said.

"She'll keep me out of her kitchen," Cristina said, "just like I always kept her out of mine."

Karl put his hand around his glass and left it there.

"I noticed you didn't put a price on Fritz's revolver," Cristina said.

"We should have buried it with him," he said.

Cristina reached across the table and touched his hand.

"You could still, you know," she said. "I would go with you."

"It's a walk," he said.

"I'll survive," she said. "Get the shovel and lantern. I'll carry the pistol."

"I'd better make sure it isn't loaded," he said.

"Don't you worry," she said. "I've done that every day since you brought it into this house."

They sneaked out the back door, passed the summer kitchen, feeling their way along the wall of the chicken coop and outhouse. Once they got beyond them, Karl fired up the lantern.

Because he did not have a free arm to support Cristina, she grasped his belt and shuffled behind him. When they reached the blacktop road, they stayed well away from the shoulder, where there were ruts and holes that could have tripped them.

"It's been a long time since we've taken a stroll together," Cristina said.

"A stroll to the cemetery in the middle of the night," he said. "I think it may be a first."

"For me," she said. "But not for you."

"I have liked it there at sunrise or sunset," Karl said. "It always gave me a sense of things coming back around."

"Are you afraid?" she asked.

"I like my independence, just like you do," he said. "I like making my own mistakes."

"Well," she said, "you've got a little experience there."

They reached the dirt road. At the end of it, beyond the lantern light, stretched the moonshadow of the big old tree near her grandparents' graves. They made their way forward, Karl using the spade like a blind man's cane.

"Tell me again why are we doing this?" he asked.

"My grandmother always said, '*Der Weg ist das Ziel.*'"

The way Cristina voiced the old saying made it sound like *Lieder*, the song a person would sing only when he finally had the distance to realize that the destination at journey's end had all along been the journey itself.

"You have always favored your grandmother, you know," he said.

"Am I really that old?" she said.

Once inside the cemetery grounds Karl stopped and put down the lantern and spade, then turned to take both of her hands in his. As he did, he felt the icy hardness of the pistol.

"You're not pointing that, I hope," he said. "I guess I should have been more careful what I said."

"You did fine," she said.

"We've got to choose a place to dig," he said.

"Why not between Fritz and Edna?" she said.

"Maybe back there under the fence line, with the barrel pointing out," said Karl.

He left the lantern with Cristina and moved forward to the edge of the light. At first he wasn't sure which fence post it was that he was looking for, the one Fritz had dropped on his shin in another century, before the logging, before Cristina, before the dynamo, before the darkness of Verdun and the Crash, the shame of Stateville, the suicides, his penitence, the letting go. Above him he could see the lights of a high-flying airliner wink a few times before disappearing into a cloud. Before modern life as they had come to know it had begun, and certainly before death. As he stood there, it all came back to him, his father's orders—where he should begin, exactly how many feet he should put between the posts, how much area to enclose. Not a square foot more than he had promised.

"I found it," he called out in the darkness. Cristina probably had no idea what he had been looking for. Many times in their life she hadn't.

He stuck the spade into the ground, then returned to her.

"Come to me," he said. "Careful. The grass is wet, but I want you near."

He picked up the lantern and took her hand. In the dark they were both unlined by time.

When they reached the spot, he left the lantern with her, then outlined with the spade a circle about a foot in diameter. Carefully, he slid the blade under the sod and lifted it in one piece like the lid of a barrel.

After placing the disk off to the side, he began digging with more determination, cutting into the rich, black dirt and piling it next to the hole. When he had gone down a foot and a half, he rested the spade against the fence post and went to Cristina.

"Do you want to do the honors?" he asked.

She held the pistol out to him by the barrel.

He got down on his knees and laid the weapon in its final resting place, where the rainwater would render it inoperable and then slowly leach away the oxides. A surge of feeling washed over him for the passing of one thing into another. He silently prayed the prayer he had prayed so often since they had taken him off to Stateville: "Lord, let me learn to love your commands."

Then he stood and shoveled the dirt back and refitted the sod, tamping it down with the sole of his shoe and feeling the moisture come up through the worn leather.

When he was done, he stood motionless for a moment.

"Are you talking to Fritz?" Cristina asked.

Karl did not realize his thoughts had made a sound.

"I was asking for forgiveness," he said.

"You've done enough of that, Karl," she said. "Let's go home now."

He took her hand.

"Why are we moving away from Abbeville, Cristina?" he said.

Through her touch it was as if he could actually feel her thoughts.

"Are you ready to risk it alone with me a while longer?" he said.

"Do you have to ask?"

"Who knows how long I'll last."

"Don't you leave me, Karl Schumpeter, wherever we go."

"You agreed to go to Betty's for my sake," he said. "And I agreed for her sake. So what about your sake, Mama?"

"I don't need much," she said.

"Well, for once you're going to have it," he said.

"Karl, are you sure?"

She gripped his hand more tightly. Maybe she was struggling to feel his unspoken thoughts, too.

"Only if you are," he said.

"I'm sure," she said.

When they got home, she disappeared into her room as Karl banked the stove and walked through the house, as he did every night, checking that all was in order—no mice in the traps, doors pulled shut against critters, lights off. As always, he finished at the bathroom door.

It was open. Drops of water in the discolored old sink told him Cristina had already finished. He shaved and washed, then checked to make sure there were no whiskers in the bowl. Then he emptied his bladder, which seemed more a matter of concentration with every passing year.

He found his way to his bedroom easily in the dark, removed his pants and shirt, and put them on the chair. Slipping out of his undershorts and t-shirt, he pulled his nightshirt on over his head, leaving his socks on his feet for warmth.

Then he felt his way to her door. She always left it open so they could hear each other breathing. But when he reached her bed, it was empty.

That was strange. He touched his way back to his room. He would have to make another walk through the house to find her.

"I'm here," she said from the direction of his bed.

"I thought you would be asleep," he said.

"Well, I hope you're not disappointed," she said.

"It's been an awfully long while," he said. "I really don't know anymore."

She reached out and found him.

"I guess we could try," he said as he felt her hand pulling him gently toward her.

"Der Weg ist das Ziel," she said.

25

WHAT IF SOMETHING HAPPENS?" MY MOTHER said when Grampa told her of their decision.

"It's just a question of where we want to be when it does," said Grampa.

"You aren't going to find it as easy as you think," my mother said.

"No," said Grampa. "I don't suppose we will."

In fact, it didn't take long before things started to go bad. First Grandma came down with a terrible case of the flu. Then Grampa had to have his gall bladder out. With each crisis we raced down to Abbeville, and my mother pressed them to move up to Park Forest like sensible people.

Much as I admired their grit, it was sad seeing them the way they were. Every visit they seemed to have slipped more.

Then the big stroke came and took Grampa in his sleep. Grandma stayed with him in bed all night and only called Henry Mueller in the morning.

"She didn't want him getting cold," Henry told my folks.

When Grandma moved in with us, it changed our lives. My mother and father ceded their bedroom to her and started sleeping in the living room on a couch that folded into a bed. I kept my room, but my mother took over part of my closet and some drawers to make space in the other bedroom for Grandma's clothes. Even though she had never before hesitated to barge in on me whenever she pleased, the new arrangement felt like an enemy occupation.

Grandma's way of coping with loss was collapse and silence. Within a month she was unable to move around on her own. My mother would have to lift her up and hold on to her as she walked.

As for me, I was mortified. The spectacle of my mother taking Grandma to the bathroom and sitting her down to do her business embarrassed me to the marrow. And my parents sleeping in the living room was a dark secret I felt I could share with no one.

Not that I didn't have other secrets. Sometimes when everybody was in bed, I pulled out selected *Life Magazines* and *National Geographics* and let the pictures bring on lovely, guilty feelings. Maybe it was a movie starlet in a revealing pose. Or an African woman wearing nothing but a few leaves over the very place I wanted most to know. Or a Polynesian girl no older than me naked to the waist the way Herman Melville described in the book my father had bought me. I didn't know what to make of the fact that the great author gave me the same feelings the pictures did; I went to that book so often that it fell open to certain pages.

At school I had felt isolated long before Grandma arrived. But with Grandma at home, I didn't dare invite anyone over. Passing between classes in the corridors, I either felt that everyone was looking at me or that I was so insignificant that no one could see me at all.

Then one day Julie Cummings stopped at my locker.

"Are you going to the Youth Center tonight?" she asked.

I shoved my jacket back inside and slammed the locker door. There wasn't anything specific I needed to hide. It wasn't like I kept in there the magazines or the book that fell open. But something about her being able to look inside made me uncomfortable and excited.

"I was just hoping I might see you," she said.

I regarded her for a moment as if I were a hundred feet away. Her lovely face. Her white blouse revealing just a hint of white elastic below. Her plaid skirt and knee socks. Anybody in school would have wanted to see her.

"Maybe," I managed to say.

"Maybe what?" she teased.

"Maybe I'll . . . maybe I'll . . ."

"See me?" she said.

Oh, how I wanted to. But I wanted to see so much more of her than I should that it was impossible for me to meet her eyes.

"Maybe I'll go tonight," I said, "if you'd like me to."

"Can't you see that I would?" she said, and with that, she twirled off into the flow of students passing between classes.

As soon as I got home, my mother went to the A&P with a neighbor. I holed up in my room and did my homework until I heard her come back. Then I went to the kitchen and idled there while she unpacked the provisions.

"Can I help you with anything?" I asked.

"That would be very nice, yes," she said.

I did what I could, choosing items whose places on the shelves I was sure of—soda, coffee, cans of soup. Heavier items were best, since they did not tremble in my hands.

"You're as jittery as a chicken that's just seen a fox," my mother said.

I couldn't tell her it had actually been an angel.

"I'm going to the Youth Center tonight," I blurted out.

My mother peeled the browned, mushy outer leaves from a head of lettuce then pushed them down into the disposal with her fingers.

"I've got the money and a ride," I said.

My mother extracted several big carrot sticks, the smudge of the earth still on them until they went under the faucet. Then the onions and celery.

"There will be plenty of adults there," I said, "so you don't have to worry."

"Not tonight, honey," she said without turning from the sink. The cold tap water splashed as she put each carrot and celery stalk under it in turn.

"I'm not some little kid," I said.

She turned up the pressure to rinse the porcelain bowl. Then she shut off the tap.

"We have to talk to Grandma's doctor," she said. "He will be at the hospital tonight. It's the only time your father and I can see him together."

She ruled my life. Everyone ruled my life but me. It was bad enough that Grandma sat there day and night threatening to give the evil eye to anybody I might want to have over. Now I had the first quality chance of happiness in my whole godforsaken life, and they were going to take it away from me.

She leaned in close to me, looked toward Grandma in the living room, and dropped her voice.

"I need you to stay with her," she whispered.

"It's not fair," I said, and I did not care who heard me.

"I think it may be important, George," she said, reaching out to bring me to her.

I turned away, banged out the back door, and left her standing there. Sad wasn't the half of it.

I crossed over into the yard of the house behind ours, then down its driveway. The field on the other side of the street lay fallow. Beyond it stood a grove of trees that stretched out along a creek.

It was not like the river where I had fished with Grampa or even like Otter Creek. Coke bottles lay in the water collecting silt. Baby Ruth wrappers furled under fallen branches like brightly colored fungi. You might even find an occasional wet, filthy sneaker left by some tenderfoot, too scared to go back and retrieve it.

I thought maybe I should just disappear into these woods forever. Forage for food. Grow wild like the animals. But that wouldn't get me to my rendezvous with Julie Cummings. I thought about sneaking out after my parents left, but what if Grandma needed me? I was trapped.

I jumped from rock to slick, shiny rock across the creek. When I reached the other side, I went straight to a tangle of branches and reeds at the base of a big old tree. It looked almost natural, beaten down as it had been by a winter of snow. The entrance to this secret place I had made for myself was just big enough to crawl through on my belly. Inside, it opened out so that I could sit upright with my back against the tree trunk and my legs stretched straight and still be hidden to the world. I eased back and reached into a hole in the trunk, where my fingers found the wax-paper package. The magazine inside was a little moist but intact.

When I opened it, I saw Julie Cummings in every nude photo. I unzipped my fly and began. When I finished, I closed his eyes and let the vile relief flow through me. I must actually have slept for a few minutes, because I came back to myself with a start. I wiped myself with leaves, pulled up the zipper, and put the magazine back in its hiding place. Then I slid out into the open air and hurried back the way I had come.

My mother was making dinner. From the smell I could tell it was going to be fish sticks. The car was in the drive, but my father was nowhere to be seen. In the bathroom, I assumed, having a cigarette with the ceiling fan on.

"Is that you, George?" my mother called.

Who else would have any reason to come into this house of misery?

"I've made dinner for you and Grandma," she said as I passed through the living room. "Brendan and I will get something on the way."

My heart sank. How much would that slow them down?

The bathroom door popped open, and my father came out.

"Well," he said, "you made it."

"Here I am," I said.

"Your mother told me about the dance," said my father. "There will be others."

With that she appeared next to him in the doorway. My father put his arm around her.

"You could ask a friend over," she said.

"Who would want to come here?" I said.

At least they did not make some phony attempt to answer. Soon I heard the ignition of the car whir and catch.

I put out dinner and ate with Grandma in silence. I had turned on the television and was able to see Huntley-Brinkley through the open doorway. She could not see it from her chair, but she did not seem to care.

I imagined the scene in the Youth Center, lights dimmed, folding chairs along the walls where people could go to make out, the faint scent of cigarettes, a stack of 45s on the changer, a slow one playing, Julie Cummings pushed up against some other guy's hard-on.

"I'm going to my room," I said.

When I got there, I found my paperback copy of *American Tragedy* and went to the place where I had left off. I would study to get the grades to get the scholarship to get to the school that would get me the job that would get me the hell out of this life.

After a while I went to check on Grandma. She wanted to move back to the living room, so I helped her to her chair next to the window. It was getting dark. I looked at my eighth grade graduation Timex and tried to figure out how long it would be before I heard the rumble and saw the lights of the car swinging into the driveway.

It was going to be too late. I knew it. At the Youth Center a record fell onto a turntable. "Tears on My Pillow." Someone's hand was on Julie's back at the place where the mysterious white strap showed through. I could not see the boy's face, but Julie's eyes were closed.

I went back to my room and pulled out my algebra book. Then I turned on the transistor radio. Dick Torcelli, the Wild One, was sending out tunes to all the kids cruising the streets looking for parties, to the kids eating hamburgers and fries in drive-in restaurants, to the couples parked in dark places. But not to losers like me.

Suddenly I heard a key in the front door. I bounded to the living room. Neither of my parents spoke. My mother went straight to Grandma.

"Let's let them be alone for a minute," my father said.

When we reached my room the Wild One was playing "Save the Last Dance for Me," and at that moment it seemed the saddest thing in the world.

"Do you want to get behind the wheel and drive me up to the Convenient?" said my father.

"I was thinking about the Youth Center," I said. "It's still early."

My father closed the door.

"Everyone is there," I heard myself say.

"I'm sorry it worked out this way for you, son," he said. "Was she very pretty?"

"Who?" I whispered.

"The one you wanted to be with."

"It was stupid even to think she could be interested in me," I said.

My father turned out the light and pulled back the curtain from my window.

"Grandma has cancer," he said. "It has spread, so there's nothing they can do."

"So she's going to die, just like Grampa did?" I said.

"Don't blame yourself, George," my father said. "You didn't know."

He cupped his hands around his eyes so he could see into the darkness. Then he motioned me over.

"Look up into the sky," he said. "When somebody dies, his energy is not destroyed. It just changes form, like soil into green growth and green growth into soil. The energy persists through eternity; you can see it glowing wherever you look."

"But it will never come back again as Grampa or Grandma, will it?" I said.

"The church says in heaven," said my father, but I knew he did not believe in church.

"I mean here on Earth," I said.

"Odds are pretty long against that," my father said.

I ENDED UP DECIDING to spend one last night in the old house in Abbeville, feeling that I had found something, or it had found me. I called to check in with Julie.

"Are you doing any better?" she asked.

"We're going to be fine," I said.

"I never doubted that," she said.

"That's why," I said. "How is Rob?"

"He's down on himself, what with school about to start."

"I'll have more time with him now," I said.

"I think that would help," she said.

"Not to mention more time with you," I said.

"Big opportunities there for being fine," she said.

Upstairs the featherbed enwrapped me like Julie's arms, and I fell asleep quickly even though it was just getting dark.

It was not a sound that awakened me but rather the absence of sound: no rumble that precedes a train, no breeze through the window, no air conditioner, no sirens, no fan. Not even a buzzing streetlamp. Surely some animals must have been on the prowl, but if they were, they moved in wild silence.

At some point I realized that my only hope of respite was to get up and walk. Outside, the moon was just beginning to rise, showing the outlines of things: the X's of the rail crossing, the tall pyramid of the church steeple. My footsteps on the macadam sounded as loud as strokes of a hammer. I did not want to awaken anyone, so I moved onto the grass where I could walk with a more nocturnal tread. I passed the empty church whose stained-glass windows a few years ago I had paid a fortune to refurbish, the preacher's house, then out beyond the edge of town, where I returned to the pavement.

When I got to the cemetery I sat with my back to Grampa's favorite tree. The moon was not in the right position, so I moved until it rose over their stone.

NOT LONG BEFORE GRANDMA went to the nursing home two girls showed up at my house early one evening unannounced. One of them was Julie Cummings, the other Judy Jameson, whose popularity had soared when she became the first in the class to get a driver's license. I was trapped.

"Hi," I said through the screen.

It was summer, and they dressed in shorts cut high on their thighs and blouses so thin I could almost see the skin beneath.

"Hi," said Julie.

"Hi," said Judy.

"Are you afraid of us or what?" said Julie.

"What?" I said, which made them laugh.

"Hiding behind the screen door like that," said Julie.

"Oh," I said. "Sure. I mean, no, I'm not afraid." I did not even convince myself.

I opened the door just wide enough to slip through.

The mosquitoes were beginning to become active. I brushed one away from my face.

"What's going on?" I asked.

"Aren't you glad to see us?" said Julie. I was afraid that if she let her glance slip down a few inches below my belt, she would have seen pointing at her the shameful physical proof of how glad I was.

"Sure," I said. "I mean, it's just kind of a surprise is all."

Judy slapped her arm, which was exposed all the way to the pit.

"I'm getting eaten alive out here," she said.

"Aren't you going to invite us in?" said Julie. This sent a shiver through me as strong as if she had asked me to invite her to my bed.

"My grandmother is in there," I explained.

"Doesn't she like you to have girls in your house?" taunted Judy.

"Everybody has a grandmother," said Julie.

She was so sweet and kind that I was afraid I might overflow right there on the sidewalk.

As I followed them in, I saw them checking everything out: the boring Great Plains landscape prints on the walls, the ridiculous old German vases on the end table, the humiliating photos of me as a baby.

"Grandma," I said, "this is Julie and Judy. They're in my class at school."

To my horror, Julie approached Grandma, reached out, and took her hand, whose skin was as dry as dead leaves.

"Nice to meet you," Julie said. "I hope we're not intruding."

"Pleased to meet you both," Grandma said.

Now the problem was where to put everybody. The kitchen was out: dirty dishes in the sink, the old scratched-up table with moisture rings all over it like an Olympic flag.

"Why don't you just sit there on the piano bench," I said.

That would put them as far from Grandma as possible, just in case any unpleasant sounds or smells emanated from her.

Julie lived in a much smarter part of the town. I had driven past her house a hundred times, wanting to walk right up and tell her why I had not met her that night at the Youth Center. But I never even stopped the car.

She moved to the piano bench. Her smooth legs rose into the tight mystery of her shorts. Her chest lifted and fell. Her face was framed by waves of hair caught in motion by hairspray as if by the shutter of a camera.

"Well," said Judy.

"What are you two going to do tonight?" I asked.

"We thought you might want to come along with us," said Julie.

It took me so much by surprise that I didn't know what to say. I looked at my watch. My mother and father were at the shopping center. I could not leave until they returned. If I knew my father, he was probably at this moment idling around the high-fi store dreaming of a new Stromberg-Carlson. When the hell were they going to get home?

"Well?" said Judy, who probably did not even have a grandmother.

"Could you give me just a few minutes?" I said. "My parents are on the way home."

"You have to actually ask them?" said Judy.

Julie leaned over and whispered something to her sharply.

"Oh, right," said Judy. "My parents make me babysit my brother. Don't you just hate it?"

What the hell was I supposed to do to keep them occupied? Play a minuet? And right after that I could suggest a game of chess. Or maybe I could just haul out my hidden collection of magazines so they could get to know my filthy soul.

"Did you hear that Annie O'Hara got pregnant?" I blurted out.

Immediately I knew it was a mistake. Grandma sat there, taking it in. Julie and Judy blushed and whispered something to one another. Hell, I didn't even have to show them the magazines.

"She's one of the sweetest people in the world," said Julie.

"Frankie pressured her," said Judy.

I didn't have any defense for Frank Lansing, who was the sort of dark, chiseled, inarticulate guy that attracted a certain kind of beautiful girl like a vacuum draws dust.

"They're sending her away," said Julie.

"I guess it would be kind of hard for her here," I said.

They looked at me as if I were the mayor of the Town Without Pity.

"We'd better go," said Judy.

"Just a few minutes more," I asked. "They've got to be here soon."

I felt pathetic.

"George?" came Grandma's voice from across the room. "Come here close."

Terrific, I thought. Now they got to hear her ordering me around like a pet.

I approached and she leaned forward.

"You know what Karl would say, don't you?" she said.

"Not really," I said.

"Why, he would have said to go," she said in a way that seemed almost girlish.

I was speechless.

"Your grandfather believed that people should never miss an opportunity for joy," she said. "I didn't always agree with him about everything, but I did about that."

"Mother would kill me," I finally managed.

"I can handle your mother," said Grandma. "I like the one you like. The one who likes you."

And for the first time since she arrived in Park Forest a smile went all the way up to her eyes.

I turned to the girls.

"Let's go," I said.

"Now?" said Julie.

"Now," I said.

A stroke took Grandma's mind before the cancer took her life. She never knew what came of that evening. I'm sure she would have been glad that Julie and I eventually married, found joy, and had a child of our own.

THE MOON STOOD ABOVE the Schumpeter stone like a crown. The air was absolutely still, as if the respiration of the earth for just that luminous moment had ceased. Then I heard a stirring above me in the boughs of the tree. I looked up and saw the eye of an owl looking down on me as if it knew something. I looked right back, because I knew something, too.

26

I LEFT ABBEVILLE EXTREMELY EARLY THE NEXT morning in order to beat the rush-hour traffic in the city. As I drove out of town, the big machines were already working the fields, their multiple headlights making them look like instruments of war. Grampa would not have recognized Abbeville today, but I had no doubt that he would have found a way to make a life in it.

When I reached home, Rob was almost ready to leave for school.

"I'll drive today," I said.

"Are you sure?" said Julie. "You've already driven a lot."

"Absolutely sure," I said.

In the car I told Rob that we were going to take a fishing trip, just the two of us.

"Fishing for what?" said Rob.

"I had exactly the same feeling when my father and grandfather took me," I said. "It's too bad you never got to meet your great-grandfather. He would have loved teaching you to cast a fly. But you'll just have to settle for me. Don't worry, though. I'll get a guide who really knows what he's doing. We'll be going to the same river I did as a boy, the one where your great-grandfather worked in a lumber camp when he wasn't much older than you are now."

"Whatever," said Rob. "Is this about me?"

"It's about both of us," I said.

And so, less than two weeks later we were on our way. We took the Indiana Toll Road through the remains of Gary and its mills. Then we got on the interstate that curved around the bottom of Lake Michigan, then headed north.

Many hours later the countryside went from flat to rolling. Eventually we left the divided highway and turned onto a two-lane road. When the fuel gauge went below a quarter of a tank I began to be a little nervous. The miles went by, up the long hills and down again, past widely spaced farmhouses and trailers on permanent foundations, but we saw nary a village or town.

"Where do people go for groceries?" I said. "Where the hell do they get gas?"

"Hey, I'm not the one who called this God's country," said Rob.

Finally we passed a shack that appeared to be a store.

"I'm hungry," said Rob.

"Let's feed the car first, okay?" I said. "If I have to call Triple A it'll take a day and half for the truck to arrive."

"You worry too much," said Rob.

The leaves in the North Woods were about to turn which meant that, thankfully, the first year of the new millennium was finally going to draw to a close. A few more months and it would be 2001, which had to be better.

"I see the motel," said Rob. "It's a real dump."

We passed it without slowing down. Other than one pickup truck with oversized wheels and antlers mounted as a hood ornament, the lot was empty. Up ahead I spotted a BP station. I pulled up to one of the pumps and filled the tank.

As we doubled back to the River's Edge Motel, I told Rob about the guide I had engaged.

"He'll help us with the entomology." I said. "The hydraulics of the river. The physics of the fly-cast."

"Don't make it seem like school, okay?" Rob said.

We pulled up at a door marked, "Office." No one was at the counter, which had scores of photos under its glass top. They came in two varieties: guys kneeling in the water, holding out fish toward the camera lens to make them look bigger, and autumnal men in camouflage holding up the heads of deer.

An old-fashioned buzzer button was mounted on the front face of the counter. "Ring," said a faded, handwritten sign, smudged by countless fingers too tired or drunk to hit the mark. When I pushed the button, I heard nothing. I pushed it again.

"It doesn't seem to work," I said.

"Yes it does," said a woman in a housedress, appearing in a doorway behind the counter. "You George Bailey?"

"How did you guess?" I said.

"Well, let's see," she said. "I only got two new reservations, and the other's already here."

She pulled open a drawer and pawed through it until she found a card, which she dealt to me face up with a practiced flick of her chunky wrist. Stay out of that game, George.

When I handed it back to her filled out, she lifted from a rack a key attached to a metal disk about half a foot across.

"Don't take it with you when you go out," she said. "Drop it off."

"It looks heavy enough to anchor a boat," I said.

"I'll need a credit card," the woman said.

"No problem," I said, finding my Visa and skidding it back to her.

She made an impression of it on an old slide machine and then had me sign for the whole amount of the reservation.

"Do you know anyplace good for dinner?" I asked.

"You'll have to go back to Chicago for that," she said, then disappeared.

I pulled the car around in front of our room, which turned out to be clean enough, though it could have used a good airing. I bridged my fingers on the mattress of one of the twin beds. It was so thin I could feel the springs. The pillow was the kind you got on airplanes. Above the small bureau, a TV was mounted high on the wall.

"This will do," I said.

I had outfitted us without any idea whether the climate would be like the Far Tortugas or the Bering Strait. Plus the waders and wading jackets the guide had said he did not provide. When I got it all inside, there wasn't much room left for Rob and me.

"Maybe we should just put some of this stuff back in the trunk," I said.

Rob plopped down on the bed nearest the TV and took charge of the remote. Clicking through the channels, he announced, "They have HBO."

I looked at the way the mattress sagged under Rob's lean frame. These were not beds for autumnal backs.

The next morning when the alarm went off in the darkness, my joints lived up to expectations, but still I got up with a real sense of excitement. I was sure Rob would feel some of the same thing if only I could wake him.

The guide's name was Johnny, and his truck, hauling a trailer-mounted float boat, crunched into the parking lot before Rob had finally pulled himself together. I went outside to greet him.

"Boy, it sure is early," I said.

"I figure you and the boy will want some breakfast," said Johnny. "There's a good little place on the way, and we've got the time."

"Hear that, Rob?" I said back into the room. "We're going to put on the feed bag."

"You two go," said Rob.

"Not a chance," I said.

Johnny was no taller than me, but he had the sturdiness of a man who pulled his weight at the oars. We stood and waited together outside the motel room door. When Rob emerged, he and I followed Johnny in my car. It seemed like miles before we pulled into the gravel lot of a little restaurant that looked as though it had never seen better days. The food turned out to be surprisingly good: pancakes and scrambled eggs and ample rashers of bacon. Even Rob gave it three and a half stars.

"We're going to be in and out of the boat a lot today," Johnny said as we ate. "This here river is generous, but don't let her fool you. She can get wild."

"Will we be shooting the rapids?" Rob asked, brightening.

"There's some white water," said Johnny.

"I've been on the river before," I told the guide. "My grandfather led the way then. He had been here back when they were logging the forests."

"You'll still see some evidence of those times," said Johnny. "Rollways where they slid the logs into the river, some abandoned rail tracks they built to get the timber from the deep woods to the rollways. Still and all, the woods have pretty much closed up over what men did to them."

When we finished, I had the waitress pour me a Styrofoam cup of the strong, black coffee she had served us at the table, and we returned to our vehicles to set off into the dark.

"Johnny seems to know what he's doing," I said as we followed him off the highway and onto a dirt road leading into the trees.

"He doesn't know enough to stay in bed until the sun comes up," Rob said.

"The early worm gets the fish," I said.

The road went from dirt to no more than two ruts through the tall grass. At some point we went down a fairly steep grade that I wasn't too sure I'd be able to get up again. Then the truck pulled to a stop, and I parked a distance behind it so Johnny would have room to maneuver the boat into the water.

"I hope you have a winch," I said.

The headlights of our vehicles made eerie shadows in the woods. I heard something move.

"Just deer," Johnny said.

He fiddled with the boat and then climbed into the truck and deftly backed the trailer down a narrow opening through the trees. As he did, I could see by the taillights the river running quickly past.

Rob and I watched as Johnny cranked the boat into the water, then let down a heavy steel anchor chain to hold it in the current as he pulled the truck and trailer back to higher ground.

"Time to suit up," he said.

I opened our trunk and handed Rob his waders.

"These are going to be baggy as hell," he said.

"If we happen upon a mermaid," I said, "she will be enchanted that you have legs, however they're clad."

I almost fell getting my foot down into the boot.

"I thought you'd done this before," Rob said.

"It was a long time ago," I said. "Here you and I meet as equals."

I pulled on a short wading jacket. A pair of sunglasses on a lanyard and an old Cubs hat completed the outfit.

Johnny, waist-deep in the river now, held the boat steady as we got into it. Then he pushed it gently into the current and hopped aboard with much more ease than I would have imagined possible for a man in boots up to his armpits.

"It's awfully dark," I said. "Will you be able to see what's ahead of us?"

"This stretch is pretty clear," he said. He handed me something heavy. "When I tell you to, push the switch and aim that lamp straight over the bow. Don't do it yet. I want you to look up over your head first."

The sky was so thick with stars that in many places they formed a seamless cloud of light.

"Look, Rob," I said.

"I am," he said.

I was listening for exasperation but heard none.

"Now turn on the lamp," Johnny said.

I fumbled for the switch, sure that if I didn't get it on in time, I'd end up impaled on a branch. When I finally succeeded, the obstruction Johnny was looking for was still twenty yards ahead. He rowed deftly around it and then told me to turn the lamp off again.

"In a few minutes the sky will start to brighten," he said. "We're out early because there are a few stretches of river that are mighty good if you are the first to get there but slow down after a bunch of folks have been slapping the water with their fly lines."

He asked me to turn on the lamp again, which I did more easily this time.

"We'll be fishing for brown trout and rainbow," he said. "In the fall the king salmon come up to spawn and die, and in the late fall and spring there are steelhead. These are big fish, gentlemen. You may see some. But I've got to tell you, give me a fat old brown on a dry fly and a four-weight rod any day."

"A dry fly is the one that floats?" I said.

"You've done this before," Johnny said.

With the sky pinking up he didn't need me to wield the lamp anymore, so I stowed it under the seat and leaned up against the gunwale to gaze into the forest we were passing through. I couldn't imagine what it must have been like when Grampa had first come here and explored places where it was possible no European had ever set foot before. I remembered the stories he told, about the bear and its cub, about the young brave spearing a fish, about how when he left, it was a wasteland as far as the eye could see.

"Your great-grandfather would have loved you, Rob," I said.

"You've said that before," he said.

Johnny leaped out of the boat and put out his hand to Rob for balance. Then to me. It made me feel a little lady-like, but at least I was able to stay upright.

He led us out into the river to a point where the water was no deeper than our knees. It surprised me that the center was so shallow. Still, moving in the current proved trickier than I remembered. Large rocks that could send you sprawling punctuated the slippery gravel on the bottom.

Johnny gave each of us a rod, placed us a distance apart, and then began to demonstrate casting technique. His line looped fore and aft, graceful as the wind in the trees. It was no wonder fish rose.

Soon Rob was throwing long, gentle loops that seemed to hang in the air and then flutter down like a leaf. The fly would drift until it was directly downstream, then he would pick it up in one movement and lay it down again, exactly the same each time. Eventually he actually got a fish on. I watched as Johnny showed him how to strip it in without using the reel. The trout turned out to be no bigger than Rob's grin.

"Now you are a man," I said.

Johnny turned his attention to me and got me to the point where I was not embarrassing myself. Still no fish came to my fly. I looked into the sliding sheet of water and saw the gravel and sand bottom, as life-less as the surface of the moon. Then Johnny put out a cast for me. Life appeared in the void, and he hooked it. He let me reel it in.

As time went by, it seemed to me that we must have chased all the fish away, but then Rob's rod bent again. With Johnny at the net he landed a pretty trout more than a foot long. As I cast over and over with no success, the lyric, "They're writing songs of love, but not for me," came into my head and I could not get it out.

The afternoon wore on. My mind went to the moving river, the cycle of the salmon, the way the forest healed itself, the rise and fall of markets. Suddenly I felt something throb at the end of my line.

"Fish on!" shouted Johnny, as if he were Melville's Starbuck.

I felt the line whine off the reel as the fish took off downriver. I did not know what to do, so I did nothing, which turned out to be just the thing.

"That's a good fish," Johnny said. "Let him run. When he jumps, bow to him. Then when he slacks off, start reeling in slow and steady."

Within a minute or two the guide made his way downstream, and suddenly the fish was in his net.

"Fourteen, fifteen inches at least," he said with authority. I waded down to see. "Nice, fat little rainbow. He just hooked himself, didn't he. They won't always be so obliging. You want to focus on your fly at all times."

As he talked, he popped the hook out of the trout's mouth. I stared at the deep, textured color of the fish until Johnny tipped the net and sent it back into the river. I followed it for a couple of feet, then it vanished.

Johnny stuck out his wet hand, and I shook it.

"Now you are a man, too," he said. "But it's time to get back into the boat."

We managed that somehow, though my way was utterly without

grace. Johnny took to the oars and put Rob in the front of the boat and me in the back so we could both cast toward shore as we floated downstream. This turned out to be a lot different from casting with both feet on the riverbed. For one thing, the boat rocked in response to every movement. For another, it was all so quick. By the time you recognized an opportunity, the current had pulled you past it. The river ran relentlessly toward the lake, where the water evaporated and made the rain that drove the underground springs that fed the river that floated the boat past fish you could not catch. History repeated, but you only got one chance.

"Fish on!" shouted Johnny.

I looked up to see Rob's rod bent almost double. The reel sang as the fish ran. Then suddenly the surface of the water shattered into a million stars as the fish flew straight upward from the deep and fell back with a mighty splash.

"That, young man, is a nice rainbow," said Johnny. "Don't try to force it. But take in line when it lets you. Whenever it isn't gaining on you, you should be gaining on it."

Rob had turned as he received this instruction. I loved the thrill in his eyes. I yearned to catch a fish like that.

"Careful, now," Johnny said. "He may have one more jump in him."

Johnny reached down into the boat and pulled up a net.

"Easy," he coaxed. "Here, I'll duck so you can get the line over me. Now reel gently until I say, then smoothly lift the rod above your head with both hands."

Rob did exactly as he was told, and the beautiful fish, streaked blood-red along its sides, came up out of the darkness and into the swooping stroke of Johnny's net.

"You've got a future as a guide, young fella," said Johnny. "You're a natural."

Rob beamed.

Marine biology perhaps, I thought. A Ph.D. from the leading university in the field and then a fellowship at Woods Hole. There were worse things a person could do, though I nurtured the hope that my son would choose something I could help him with.

"What a fish!" I shouted.

"Let's get a picture," said Johnny, handing a point-and-shoot to me.

Johnny pulled the fish up out of the net and held it out in front of Rob while I proudly recorded his victory.

"Everybody sit down now," said Johnny. "We're coming up on a little bit of a rough patch."

The boat began to bounce and tip and thud off rocks. I put the rod between my knees and took hold of the gunwales.

Johnny was paddling madly now, holding the boat back as he maneuvered around the bigger rocks. On one side of the river the bank rose almost vertically a couple hundred feet. Suddenly it wasn't Michigan at all. It was the western wilderness. Rob whooped. I held on so hard my hands ached.

Soon we were in softer water again. Johnny lightened up on the oars.

"You okay, Rob?" I called.

He turned around.

"That was dope," he said. I did not like the word, but I had to admit that I had felt a rush myself.

"You're going to have another ride down below here a piece," said Johnny. "It's a little hairier, as a matter of fact. Up above it are some pretty good lies. We'll stop and do some fishing before attempting it."

"I have total confidence in you," I said.

Johnny turned around again and looked at my hands.

"I guess then you can let go of the boat," he said.

We drifted through a stretch of water as flat as a mirror. Johnny dipped an oar in from time to time to make subtle adjustments. Rob and I laid out our lines and let our flies dead-drift alongside us in the current. But nothing rose.

"It's all sand in here," said Johnny. "Just get some casting practice in, 'cause you won't be catching nothing. Up ahead's where we'll find Moby Dick."

"What's with all the suds?" Rob asked, pointing to foam that gathered in a backwater. "Did somebody dump detergent in the river?"

"They better not," said Johnny, "or they'll have about a hundred guides coming after them. But don't worry. The foam don't mean nothing. It's just nature blowing bubbles."

The boat picked up speed until Johnny had to work the oars continuously to keep it headed straight. A few hundred yards farther on he let loose the anchor chain, which went down with the roar of a sea monster.

He went over the side as easily as a man dismounting a horse. Rob was next. I got one heavy, awkward boot over the side, then found myself hopelessly stuck. I leaned outward, feeling for the river bottom or a rock that would give me some purchase. There was nothing but ceaseless motion.

"Here," said Johnny. "Put your hand on my shoulder."

Rob looked on in amusement. With one feeble push I was free. My boot found something that seemed solid. But it wasn't. I was ready for the shock of cold water, but Johnny held me upright by my suspenders like a marionette.

"Careful there, partner," he said.

He led us a bit downstream of the drift boat, reminding us to take small, careful steps and keep right behind him.

"Pretty good vertical drop along here," he said. "There's a deep pool ahead that always holds good fish."

It lay about twenty yards downstream. The current poured over the rocks along the right bank and into a black boil no more than six feet out from where we stood.

"If you do tie into a fish here," Johnny said, "you've got to stand your ground. Follow it down too far, and you'll go in over your head."

Johnny placed himself below Rob and me near where the gravel dropped off. I secured myself by jamming my left foot between two big rocks and bracing my right leg against a boulder. The river surged around my knees, making intricate patterns of turbulence like clouds from a satellite.

My first cast fell way short. But after a few minutes, I began putting the flies into the right general area. Much good it did me. The best I could offer summoned absolutely no response from the deep.

Patience has never been my strong suit, but I soon forgot everything but the 10 A.M. and 2 P.M. arc of the fly rod, the eddies and runs of the current, the drift of the fly.

Which suddenly vanished.

I lifted my rod to bring it back to the surface—and something surged at the end of the line.

"Don't even think about touching that reel," said Johnny.

The fish raced downstream, taking line. Soon I was afraid I would lose this magnificent creature, which now loomed as large to me as love.

I started to wade after it, stumbling on rocks, moving faster than I was comfortable with, propelled by the force of the current.

"Watch yourself there, partner," said Johnny. "Ain't a fish in this river worth dying for."

I managed to slow the fish and myself down and turned sideways to the flow to reduce its pressure on me. I took a lateral step, reeling in slack until I felt the shuddering terror on the other end of the line.

"Put some wood to it," said Johnny. "There's no two ways about it: If you don't gain on it, it'll gain on you."

"That's two ways right there," I said.

"Win or lose. Live or die," said Johnny. "Eat or be eaten."

I took one more step downriver onto a rock, but when I lifted my upstream boot, the rock gave way. Water poured into my waders, then closed over my head. Something stronger than anything I had ever felt in my life pulled me down.

I managed to fight it until I got my head above the surface for an instant. I gulped in air, but water came with it, and when I went down again, I was struggling so hard that I coughed beneath the surface, which brought even more into my lungs.

My eyes opened and I saw far above me the bright, living, inaccessible sky. Then suddenly some terrible creature grabbed hold of me as if to tear my head from my body. I struggled against it. But it was no use. I went limp. At that very moment I felt something levitating me until I broke the surface.

"You're all right now," Rob said. "Just let your feet down. It's shallow here. We're still above the rapids. You're safe."

I was coughing when I felt the bottom under one heel. Rob's arm beneath my chin let go, and I came to a standing position. The water in my boots was so heavy I could barely move.

Rob stood next to me.

"I hope I didn't hurt you," Rob said. "They teach you that you have to be pretty physical to overcome a person's panic."

"You saved my life," I said.

"I guess I did, didn't I," said Rob.

I dragged my boots toward shore. They grew heavier and heavier the more my body came out of the water.

"Let's get up on the bank and pour those waders out," said Johnny, who had finally reached us. "Hell, there might even be some fish in them."

"First take this one," said Rob.

He handed me my rod, and on the end of the line another miracle. The fish was still there.

"That's some pretty fine work there, son, saving the man, the rod, and the fish," said Johnny.

The trout was as exhausted as I was and succumbed easily. When it was close to shore, Johnny seized it by the tail and lifted it out of the water. It was a behemoth.

"That's one fat brown trout," he said. "I'd say twenty-four inches easy."

As Johnny revived the fish, I got up on the bank, took down the suspenders of my waders, and pulled the Gore-Tex away from the wet denim of my jeans.

"You really showed me something today, young man," Johnny said to Rob.

"First time for everything, I guess," said Rob.

He was on the bank now with me.

"In my boat," said Johnny, "keeping somebody afloat is about the best thing a person can do."

As I climbed out of my waders, Johnny sat talking to Rob. Across the river two great pines towered above all the rest.

"Look at the eagles," Johnny said, pointing into the cloudless sky where a pair of them glided like passing jets.

I watched as one great bird came closer and closer, then landed in the nearer of the trees. The branches shuddered. Then the other eagle found the second tower.

"That's a sight you don't see in the city," Johnny said.

The breeze was cool on my wet clothes, but the sun warmed me. I looked down at a line of bubbles in the river, the current bearing them ceaselessly onward, bits of nature's passing foam.